SPIES

Sonia Baranikowa.

SPIES

By
THEA VON HARBOU
AUTHOR OF "METROPOLIS"

Translated from the German by
HELEN J. STIEGLER

With 12 Illustrations

NEW YORK : LONDON
G. P. PUTNAM'S SONS
The Knickerbocker Press
1929

CONTENTS

CHAPTER		PAGE
I.—Number 326		3
II.—Haghi		30
III.—The Pistol-Shot at the Olympic		46
IV.—The Spider in His Web		68
V.—The Russian Tea		85
VI.—The Devil Drives		97
VII.—A Descent into Hell		117
VIII.—Kitty		143
IX.—From a Prison Cell		155
X.—Number 326 Reports		167
XI.—Sentenced		180
XII.—"As Ye Sow"		189
XIII.—The Package in the Mail		194
XIV.—The Treaty		201
XV.—The Last Commission		217
XVI.—Nemo-the-Clown		227

iii

CONTENTS

CHAPTER   PAGE

XVII.—33 133 236

XVIII.—THE WRECK 245

XIX.—REVELATIONS 258

XX.—RUN TO EARTH 265

XXI.—THE TAKING OF THE BANK . . . 273

XXII.—POISON GAS 280

XXIII.—THE FINAL CLUE 293

XXIV.—THE LAST PERFORMANCE . . . 301

EPILOGUE 306

ILLUSTRATIONS

PAGE

SONIA BARANIKOWA . . . *Frontispiece*

HE HELD UP THE PICTURE TO HER AS THOUGH
IT WERE A MIRROR—A FIENDISH LOOKING
GLASS 39

NUMBER 326 CAUGHT HER IN HIS ARMS AS THE
GUN SLIPPED FROM HER HAND . . . 53

"DO TRUST ME," HE BEGGED. "LET ME HELP
YOU" 91

HE THREW A CARELESS GLANCE AT THE MONEY,
THEN RESUMED HIS ADMIRING ATTENTION . 121

SHE EXTENDED HER HANDS TO THE RADIANT HEAT 149

"WE CANNOT AFFORD TO HAVE EITHER AN ARREST
OR A SCANDAL" 185

HE HEARD THE VERDICT AND ACCEPTED IT WITH-
OUT A QUESTION 213

SCREAMS OF AGONY TURNED THE TUNNEL INTO
AN INFERNO 249

WITH AN EAR-SPLITTING ROAR THE COCOANUTS
EXPLODED 269

v

ILLUSTRATIONS

PAGE

THE DOOR SWUNG SUDDENLY OPEN ON SILENT HINGES. . . . A SHADOW FELL ACROSS THE WALL 285

STUNNED, THEY HAD SURRENDERED WITHOUT RESISTANCE 295

vi

SPIES

I

SPIES

CHAPTER I

NUMBER 326

"NUMBER 326 is here, sir," announced Vincent, in his weak, throaty voice.

The Chief of the Secret Service arose from behind his desk like an ominous thunder cloud. His heavy face, with its undershot jaw and protruding underlip, bespoke the bulldog tenacity for which he was famous. From beneath his beetling eyebrows he glared at the door, which, with a silent gesture, he ordered the secretary to open.

On the threshold, his arms in the grasp of two police-officers in uniform, stood a disreputable figure, clad in rags of filth,— unkempt, unshaven and foul. The Chief's frown relaxed at this sight. At a signal from him, the two released their holds, and the seeming tramp stepped into the room, Vincent closing the double door behind him.

3

A close observer might have followed beneath the dirty scrubble on his face the outlines of the firm, square jaw, and any who looked at him, as he abandoned his vagabond slouch and raised his eyes boldly, could not fail to recognize the true man beneath this sordid exterior.

That the bold eyes were themselves observant, was quickly evident. As he waited for the Chief to speak, they saw Vincent, with a furtive movement, slide his hand across his chest toward the lapel of his coat. The next instant, and the attendant was catapulted across the room, the recipient of a terrific upper-cut from Number 326, and crashed against the Chief's heavy desk, before which he collapsed like a bundle of old rags.

Chief Jason's face purpled with astonished rage at this sudden assault upon his trusted secretary, but before he could even begin to utter the explosive words that burst to his lips, Number 326, with the spring of an angry tiger, had leaped upon the prostrate form of the half-stunned man, and despite Vincent's efforts, had stripped from the buttonhole of the lapel a tiny camera.

"Well—! a bit queer," commented Number 326, with a wry smile. "Just to get things clearly before us:

I go away for two years, because my face is becoming too well known— I return— I find your code message — according to orders I hide myself in the slums, let my beard grow, forget that water was made to wash with— adopt these filthy rags— play communist at the water-front— am promptly arrested as planned— only to be secretly photographed in this disguise in *your* own private office and by *your* own secretary."

As he spoke, he held out, on a palm that had known neither soap nor water for days, the infinitesimal instrument, a marvel of delicate precision, and gazed at his superior with a whimsical look of reproach upon his dirty and unshaven face. A moment of intense silence ensued, as the Chief stood bewildered, turning the tiny camera over and over in his hands.

The office in which this episode had occurred was, in many respects, a curiosity, and earned many a well meant reproach.

"Look here, old man," his best friend had volunteered on one occasion after considerable whiskey-and-soda, "I know there is no ordinance requiring the head of our Secret Service to be a man of artistic taste, or restricting his right to decorate his office as he sees fit, but you take unfair advantage of this loophole in our statutes. Haven't you any sensibilities yourself,

/ or at least some consideration for the unfortunates who come to this office to see you? How can you stand having these idiotic gods grinning in your face all day long — to watch those simpering muses and inane graces chase themselves over your walls from morning till night— not to mention that marathon runner over there, who incidentally must have been in rotten form. Let me get together with some of the other fellows and clean out this mess. I'll bet you'll be cured of your dyspepsia— and a lot of your vile temper— within a week."

But Miles Jason had good reasons of his own for not parting with the ornate and ugly tapestries, and with the numerous bad bronzes that cluttered up his office. Those inanely grinning gods concealed the most intricate instruments, which registered with absolute accuracy any stress of emotion or sensation of any person who entered the room, recording and analyzing subconscious reactions with infallible and undeviating clarity; the subject remaining in total ignorance of the observation. The body of that futile marathon runner, for instance, contained a sound detector of such supreme delicacy that it amplified the heart-beats of anyone approaching it so that they became plainly audible in the outside recording room—

the rhythm and speed of the beats bearing witness to the mental attitude of the subject.

The events that followed that moment of silence after Number 326 had spoken threw the complicated mechanism completely out of order for some moments, by dint of the brutal volume of sound poured into it; and the photographic record proved but a series of indistinct blurs, so rapid was the action.

The Chief was obviously struggling with himself to accept an unbelievable fact— something which could not be possible. A movement on the floor aroused him. He dropped his eyes from the tiny camera to the pitiful remnant of a man that lay at his feet, pressing a blood-flecked handkerchief to his mouth and fighting for breath between coughs. And when Vincent, slowly raising his head, looked at his Chief with an unmistakable sneer on his face, a roar like that of an enraged bulldog burst from Jason's throat, and he hurled himself at the man. Clutching him by the shoulders with a grasp of steel, he dragged the traitor to his feet, and with the fury of a maniac shook him wildly— worried him as a dog worries a helpless foe.

"In whose pay are you, you damned scoundrel?" he bellowed, "who is paying you to double-cross me, you dirty rat?" His terrible arms continued to hurl the man violently from side to side, as if he were trying to shake an answer from that sneering mouth.

Number 326 had seated himself calmly, with his filthy hands between his knees, and was watching, with a strange mixture of pity, curiosity, and admiration for Vincent's dogged courage, this brutal handling of the man who had tried to outwit him and whose futile attempt had brought upon himself this horrid fate.

Vincent looked like Death— a ghastly, grinning Death, convulsed with mirth. For his emaciated body seemed in truth to be racked less by Jason's violence than by the spasms of almost hysterical laughter that broke from him. His blood-shot eyes glared into the distorted face of his Chief with a sneering hatred, trying with exultant vindictiveness to compensate themselves, ere it was forever too late, for every look of submission and subservience that they had given in the past. His refusal to answer seemed due less to obstinacy than to his complete absorption in this orgy of visual vengeance, which fired him to a state of ecstacy.

"Who is it? Who— who— who—!" roared Jason, hurling out the words over and over again in his blind fury, as though they were the only ones left in his vocabulary. "WHO— WHO?"

"You can— keep— that— up— as— long— as— you— like," gasped Vincent, half choked, with foamy blood dripping from his mouth, and his emaciated body sagging like that of a martyr who has been broken on the rack. He bared his teeth in a vicious snarl.

"Keep on asking 'who— who'! You can tear my arms out, or shake what's left of my lungs out of my body, but you'll never shake an answer out of me! Why don't you keep it up? 'Who— who— who—'?" The jeering voice was cut off, by a racking cough that in turn was choked by a horrid gurgle. As Jason with a shudder released him, the traitorous aide sank to the floor, with the blood gushing from his mouth. And Number 326, still watching calmly, like a spectator at a show, saw clearly that it was not merely the sight of the blood gushing from the sick man that had made the Chief release him; it was more than that, it was the realization of the indomitable will that he would not be able to break, of the fanatical stubbornness of this fragile man— a man who, supported by the knowledge that he was dying, was immune to threats or to terrors, certain of sure and imminent release.

"Damn it!" muttered Jason, to himself, "he's like all the others, only worse!" His fingers fumbled for an electric button on his desk. His eyes remained fixed upon the doomed man— the man he had trusted, and who had betrayed him. Two husky officers entered. Either one alone could have lifted Vincent with one hand and have carried him away. The Chief nodded toward the man on the floor. "Place him under arrest," he said bitterly.

The two picked up Vincent, who offered no resistance. Supported by them, he staggered toward the door.

"Vincent," snapped the Chief. The three halted, and the man addressed turned his head defiantly. His eyes were filled with the blazing hate of those of a wolf. "Vincent," continued Jason, his voice quivering in the chagrin of his defeat, "you are a doomed man. Perhaps you are leaving some one behind whom you'd like taken care of. That person or persons will reap tremendous benefits if you will give me the name of the man who has bribed you to double-cross me and to spy on me."

The eyes of the dying man stared their insolent refusal, and a spiteful grin twisted his bloody mouth. "Find him yourself," he jeered, "and," with a half-pitying look at Number 326, he added, "God help *you* when you do!"

Number 326 rose to his feet and bowed. "Thanks," he said, "perhaps He will."

"I'll speak about it when I get to Heaven," replied Vincent, sardonically. "Good-bye, Chief, I'm sorry you let little things upset you so, for that's all I am, a little thing— wait till you run into the big ones." And, with a final sneer, he staggered from the room, the heavy door closing with a thud behind him and his escort.

"Well—?" said Number 326, in quiet interest, "what's it all about?"

The Chief stared at him, for a moment forgetting the scenes of the past few minutes. No wonder this man was the best of his operatives. Nothing seemed to ruffle or to disturb him— to break that unvariable calm. And it came again to Jason, that much as he had used him, he knew practically nothing about the man. Some years before, he had appeared, faultlessly dressed, showing every sign of culture and breeding, and if not wealth certainly something near it,— had presented credentials from the highest sources and had requested a position in the Service. The credentials, although undisputably genuine, pointedly omitted any name, and the young man had, upon being asked, remarked, with equal pointedness, that he had supposed that Secret Service men were known only by numbers. It was very irregular, but the letters he bore left the Chief no option, and Number 326 was duly sworn in.

There had never been occasion to regret it upon the part of Headquarters. Fearless, a glutton for work no matter how unpleasant, keen, always cool and collected, he had rapidly risen to be the most valuable man in the Service. And, still, to the Chief he remained only Number 326, about whom nothing was known, except that he lived, when in the city, at one of the best hotels— that he kept his man-servant and a handsome car, and that he never suffered for lack of money. He seemed to avoid women, though with some difficulty. A most presentable young man, with comfortable means at his disposal, does not always find that easy. He did not drink, except most occasionally, and he never gambled. When twitted about the last, he had remarked that he enjoyed sufficient gambling when on the job, and played for stakes that made those bet at the card-table seem somewhat tame.

Such was Number 326. "Too good to be true," Jason had often thought. "When he breaks, he is going to break badly."

"Well," repeated Number 326, who had, through

the long silence, steadily met the Chief's stare, "well—whom is he talking about?"

The reiterated question snapped Jason from his thoughts, and, in fact, seemed an electric spark which kindled his wrath anew. His face flamed again, and his penetrating grey eyes narrowed under the heavy brows.

"If I knew that," he fumed, "would I have to bother with you? If I knew that, would we be the laughing-stock of everyone— the butt of every comic sheet— material for any yapping editorial writer in his filthy paper. . . . ? I . . . . by Heaven and the seven little fishes, 326, you've GOT to find this man for me. No, it's not a man— it's a fiend— a monster— an invisible beast! And you're going to stalk it, and track it to its lair, and shoot it down, or get shot down yourself! Do you understand me, sir?"

"Not a word," smiled Number 326 through his disfiguring growth of stubble and dirt. "I gather though that you are somewhat excited over someone. Let's hope you can calm down enough to tell me about it."

Jason glowered at the young man, and then, slowly, the flush left his face as his anger receded. As he looked down at the disreputable figure, for Number 326 had returned to his chair, a light of admiration crept into the hard eyes, and an expression of affection softened the ugly face.

"Of course you don't understand— how could you? I'm an ass, and a damned rude one. This is no way to greet you. Welcome back, boy." He held out a huge paw. "Did you have a great time— fine trip— good weather—?"

"Thanks," laughed the young man. "No apologies— I may not understand what you are talking about, but I do understand *you,* Chief. Yes, we had rather good weather over *there,* but you seem to be in a bit of a fog *here.* As far as I can grasp, you're after a man, or men, of whose identity you are quite uncertain, and whose whereabouts are a mystery.— Yet there must be some people who do know. . . . . ."

"There are," interrupted the Secret Service Chief in a sour voice, "and a whole lot more of them than suit us; but we can't get their mouths open— they can't be made to talk."

"None of them?"

"Not a single damned one of them! Whether fear or a fanatical loyalty keeps their mouths shut, we don't know,— but keep them shut they all do. We have clapped those we have caught in padded cells, handcuffed, and guarded like the Crown Jewels, only to have them die mysteriously before our very eyes *in* their cells. Several who were showing signs of weakening, and who might have talked, fell over dead as though the bare thought had killed them. Some have committed suicide when they felt they couldn't hold out any longer— in mortal terror lest they should be forced to give away their secrets. A man to arouse one's envy, boy,— that man we want for having the magnetism to inspire such magnificent loyalty, or the power to awaken such fear, that his creatures are ready, and willing, to give up their lives rather than his secrets,— to die rather than to betray him!"

His troubled eyes wandered sadly to the door that had so recently closed behind the latest captured henchman of this invisible Power. "That one," he added, nodding to the door, "actually rejoices in the thought of approaching death because it will release him from the possibility of turning traitor."

"Turning traitor to whom?"

"*That,* my lad, is what *you* are going to find out for me."

Number 326 made no reply except a quizzical smile, and his unusually expressive eyes rested with quiet patience on his Chief's face.

SPIES

Jason sat down at his desk, and, with his foot, pressed a concealed lever beneath it. Immediately, the room, instead of being all ears, became deaf and blind. The Olympic gods ceased their automatic watchfulness, and closed their mechanical ears and eyes, much to the relief of the overworked staff in the recording rooms. The Secret Service head preferred to talk to Number 326 unheard.

"My message to you was urgent because I have a strong belief that, after a short spell of inactivity, they are about to start working again."

"Doing just what?" queried Number 326.

"Better ask me what *not*," snorted Jason. "Robberies, assaults, hold-ups, murders, every sort of killing, swindle, treason, blackmail, and whatever else you can think of in the way of crime! Mind you, I don't even *know* whether we are dealing with a small gang, or with a great secret organization— a Mafia, a Ku Klux Klan — or with a vicious political faction that will stop at nothing to gain its ends. But there *must be a directing head*— a Master Mind! We have no idea who this may be; we have not the slightest suggestion of what he looks like; nor have we the faintest clue to where he may be found. In fact, we know only one thing with certainty— and that is we know nothing at all.

"The local crimes are bad enough, God knows, still they affect us, and us only. They seem to be mainly for the purposes of revenge and loot— money to give power to the devil who must be at their head. But the time has come when we've *got* to put an end to their activities, and quickly, or the world will have another war on its hands."

"Just why?"

"My boy, it is fully as important, if not more so, for the sake of peace between nations that each does not know every thought and plan of the other, as it is for the sake of peace between families, even though they be the best of friends. This devil is threatening that peace. Our State secrets have become mere trading papers; and it's little consolation to know that we have the privilege of purchasing the proffered secrets of other nations. Locks and safes have become empty words. It's an old saying that walls have ears, but now walls have, in addition, camera-eyes and microphones with long distance connections that could serve as models for the public telephone companies. There is no longer such a thing as a State 'secret'! Within the hour, or even less of their ratification, even though it has taken place in a subterranean bank vault, the contents of supposedly secret pacts and treaties are in the hands of the very people for whom they are least intended. Statesmen transferring important documents are waylaid going from one embassy to another, are assaulted, are robbed of their papers— and the perpetrators vanish into thin air. Steel walls have turned into glass, paper has become transparent, doors no longer boast locks. Crimes of every sort are committed and remain un-atoned for; no one can discover who committed them. As I said, the few we have been able to arrest won't open their mouths— or they die; which amounts to the same thing as far as we are concerned.

"There's the situation, and it's a rotten one. I tell you it's turning my hair grey! Will you try your hand at it?"

"Why ask that, sir?" replied the young man, looking the other squarely in the eye.

Jason returned the look. He swallowed, and cleared his throat. "I knew perfectly well what your answer would be, my lad. There was no offence meant. It was my duty to ask. Let me show you why; and don't pledge yourself until you have seen."

He went to a heavy steel cabinet, and, opening a drawer which was triple-locked, lifted out a thick volume. He remained standing, looking grimly at the book, and his face seemed to age with grief. After a moment of this silent contemplation, he turned to Number 326.

"Stand up," he said sternly. "It is sacrilege to remain seated in the presence of this record. Come here!"

He began to turn the pages slowly, one by one, as Number 326 followed with his eyes. Each page bore the photograph of a man, and beneath each picture was a number. A few terse remarks were written in the margins:

"Number 17. Found shot. No clue.

"Number 256. Stabbed to death. Slayer arrested. Refused to talk. Suicide by poison before second hearing.

"Number 53. Found shot. No clue.

"Number 118. Found violently insane. No explanation.

"Number 164. Suicide, reason unknown. Last messages undecipherable.

"Number 90, Disappeared Sept. 25th. Fate unknown.

"Number 193. Burned to death in hotel fire. Door locked on *outside*.

"Number 115. Drowned. Evidence of violence. No clue.

"Number 208. Found shot. No clue.

"Number 259. Automobile accident. Car went over cliff. Steering - knuckle broken. Found to have been sawed more than half through."

"And so forth," said the Chief sadly, shutting the book. He smiled grimly into Number 326's flushed and indignant face which was twitching with sympathy. "A pretty record," he continued bitterly, "and if I had included every casualty it would be a much longer one. But to pander to our own feelings we have entered many a doubtful case in other records. This list is long enough as it is to require my asking you my question. Are you now willing to accept this assignment— an assignment that certainly is more than dangerous, and in which the chances are more than great that you will meet with an unexplained and unavenged death?"

Number 326 raised his steady eyes to his Chief. "I thought I had already answered, sir." He reached for the book, turned over its pages slowly, and then, closing it softly, pressed his hand on it as if to stamp it with his oath of allegiance to the dead men who had gone before him. There was something sacramental in the quiet action, and for a moment the stern eyes of Miles Jason blurred.

"And not *one* of these men left a single clue behind him?" asked Number 326 suddenly. "Not a single written word— code message or note of any sort?"

"No— not the slightest clue," answered the Chief, and the words puckered his mouth like alum. "At least, *we* never found any."

"Hm! Interesting," observed Number 326, thoughtfully.

"Yes! But damned annoying," retorted Jason. "I tell you it's a problem over which a man can lose his life or his reason, if not both, and it *is* turning my hair grey!"

"Well, Chief," said Number 326, with a quick smile, "I'll endeavour to keep both. Now, let's have the instructions, for the sooner I get to work the better."

"There aren't any instructions, I haven't any to give. Do the best you can— that's all I can tell you, and even that's superfluous. Make all reports in code. We'll change every third day. No telephoning, of course. Telegrams to General Delivery #30. My letters to you will bear the usual pin-prick in the upper right hand corner. Have you your identification disk? Good. Complete authority will be formally assigned to you, but don't wait for that. Leave here by the secret exit. And keep me informed where I can reach you at all times."

"That last won't be easy, Chief, but I'll try. At present, when I'm not, under your orders, a dirty bum of a wharf-rat, I am Mynheer Voostenwalbert Schimmelpenninck from Amsterdam residing with his valet Franz at the Olympic Hotel, suite 119-120."

"*What* was that name," exclaimed Jason.

"Mynheer Voostenwalbert Schimmelpenninck," replied Number 326, with a grin. "I picked that out very carefully— I'm sorry you don't like it. You see if anyone tries to talk about me the listener will think the speaker is queer and that may save gossip.

"Why, Chief, I'll have probably at least ten different addresses— on the waterfront, in the Ghetto, with the Salvation army, and with the Devil and his grandmother. Maybe my headquarters will be in that unfinished tunnel for the railroad that went broke. That's ideally situated for my purposes. It's near enough to the city, grass is growing knee-high in the abandoned tracks, and little grey cats go there on successful mouse hunts. I like cats. And mice.

The pursuers as well as the pursued— Which feeling is likely to bring about complications. I say, Chief, won't anything make you smile?"

The older man did not answer. He looked steadily at Number 326, and held up his hand in a deprecating gesture, which the latter did not deign to notice.

"Cheer up, we'll get them," he continued briskly, as he shook his Chief's hand. "I'm off now. No wait a second— I'll write down my name for you and if you want me get in touch with Mynheer Schimmelpenninck's valet. He worships his master with a curious mixture of devotion and adoration. He's a jewel without price, and faithful beyond description."

Miles Jason did not seem to hear. His face was troubled.

"326," he exploded suddenly, "do you happen to be in love?"

"Most certainly not, sir," replied the young man emphatically.

"Then there's not much chance of your getting married for the present— not for several months?"

"There surely is not, Chief. No married bliss for me. I'm too busy having a good time on the job with the Service to have any time for the deadly female of the species in any way."

"Good— that relieves my mind a little. I've always felt the same way. But, generally speaking, I haven't the slightest objections to my men getting married; in fact, it seems good for them— makes them more ambitious. Love is a great driver, and a wife who wants more money just about as great. Good for the office morale, too,— it's the married men who keep steady and on the job. That is if they don't go to the other extreme. But, my boy, this detail you're on is not the job for a married man or one who's thinking of getting married. I'm relieved.

"The damned job has created enough widows already, and," he continued bitterly, "they all turn to me for help! Want me to get their husbands back for them. Probably had little enough use for them when they were alive, at that. Haven't you noticed how many wives have sour faces? But no sooner are the husbands dead or missing, than they suddenly discover how much they had loved them, and are inconsolable in their grief.

"And then, there's another kind. Take the widow of Number 90— the one who disappeared. That poor devil is without doubt deader than Moses, but you can't make that woman believe it. She comes here regularly, at least once a week, and demands

24

that I give her man back to her, or deliver his corpse. As I can't do either, she refuses to believe he's dead. And she holds me responsible for his disappearance! I tell you that woman has a most uncanny faith in her conviction, and it's contagious. Why I'm almost expecting to see him show up some fine day, yanked out of Heaven itself by her persistence. Even if Number 90 doesn't show up till Judgment Day, and if his widow and I happen to be standing there together, she'll point him out to me and shout 'didn't I tell you? I *knew* he wasn't dead!'

"Then there's the widow who wants to be paid for the loss of her dead man. She charges into the office with a young army of children, and in the belief that I don't take the trouble to count them, increases the number from time to time. Our ears get filled with harsh words about neglected widows and orphans, but the roaring torrents of a Niagara are blissfully silent compared with the torrents of abuse that those female tongues can hurl at us.

"Then, there are those women who remain absolutely quiet. They come for news of their husbands, and when I'm forced to tell them— 'Madam, it's rotten, damnably rotten, but your husband has been killed,' they don't say a word. They sink down in a chair, and

just stare blankly. They're the worst of the lot—
I can get mad at the others. If you had a wife, boy,
she'd be that kind."

"We seem to be a pair of misogynists, Chief," replied Number 326, chuckling at this tirade, "so you
needn't worry about being pestered by either my
wife or my widow." Gratefully, the Chief gripped his
hand.

A short time later, Number 326 emerged from the
shelter which protected a hole in the pavement a
full street away from Headquarters— this, for the
time being serving as exit number 8/x/7. In front of
it sat a laborer quietly munching his mid-day meal. He
scarcely raised his eyes, as Number 326, pushing his
shabby hat to the back of his head, shoved his hands
deep into his tattered pockets, and ambled leisurely
down the dirty street like a man who had all the time
in the world to kill. But as the Secret Service operative turned the corner, the laborer arose, and made his
way toward the tobacco-store opposite— the store
showing a telephone sign.

Much to the satisfaction of Number 326, he did
not arouse the special interest of any of the police

whom he encountered. Several of them who seemed a bit curious he threw quite off their guard by the disarming friendliness of his smile. On, through more and dirtier streets he passed, till he reached the drab alley in which he had been living. It was blind, and flanked by decrepit tumble-down houses that looked more as if they harboured spectres than humans. Groups of pallid little Jewish children were listening to a noisy street organ, their great eyes reflecting the wisdom of the ages, their pinched faces old with much unnecesary knowledge and useless sophistication. A wooden-legged man was grinding the organ with great gusto.

The ramshackle house, in which, high up under the roof, Number 326 rented an attic room, looked for all the world like a mangy porcupine, with its many chimneys sticking crazily from the roof. Rachel Goldbaum, the landlord's daughter, was leaning against the filthy doorway. With the early oriental ripeness her heavy, dark eyes already smouldered with suppressed fires. A smile— an invitation— curved her full red lips, as the languorous eyes came to rest on the frank countenance of the tenant of her meanest attic room. Number 326 gave her a friendly nod as he passed. She returned it with a forlorn smile. Appropriately enough, the organ-grinder wheezed out the "Song of the Evening Star."

Just as Number 326 started to pass in front of him, a woman's shriek rent the air— a penetrating cry of terror, which seemed to issue from one of the dirty windows across the street. Number 326 stopped abruptly, throwing his head back in keen attention, listening for the cry again that he might rush to the aid of the poor tortured creature, and rescue her from the brute who was the cause of it. But the cry was not repeated. Everything was silent, except for the wheezing of the horrible organ which the one-legged grinder turned ceaselessly.

A few hours later, while, high in his attic room, Number 326 was peacefully sleeping away the afternoon hours, with his alarm clock set for eight o'clock, the film which the one-legged organ-grinder had taken of him as he waited for the repetition of that cry of terror was being shown in the projection-room of his unknown adversary. Considering the unfavorable light conditions under which it had been taken, it was most successful, revealing in close detail all of the young tramp's identifying characteristics, except-

ing that tiny scar over his left eyebrow——the reminder of a college fracas.

The film more than made up for the earlier failure of Vincent, whose capture had been reported within ten minutes of its effect, and whose fate seemed a matter of indifference to the sinister figure that studied minutely the enlarged picture on the screen before him.

CHAPTER II

HAGHI

HAGHI's Bank was one of the more recent buildings and perhaps the most handsome and imposing one in the old fashioned and ugly city. That, as a bank, it had achieved the position it now held, was a phenomenon; that one man was responsible for this was even a greater one, considering the man.

He had come to the city a few years before, unknown and unheralded, yet the certified drafts upon several of the richest financial institutions in Europe which he brought with him proved that here was another silent multi-millionaire. In a strangely short time, his millions opening the way for him, he had established himself as one of the leading financiers of the country, not only as president of his own bank, but as director of half a dozen others, and chairman of numberless boards, none of which could afford not to avail themselves of his astounding ability and his uncanny judgment, or fore-knowledge, of future events in international relations.

And yet, not only was this man a cripple, confined to his wheel-chair by his paralyzed legs, but nothing was known about his antecedents nor his nationality. Evidently a foreigner, but from where? "I am a citizen of the World," he would reply to the question. Perhaps, a Russian? He spoke the language perfectly, but he was equally at ease with many others. However, the fact that he looked not unlike Lenin lent favour to this supposition.

His infirmity seemed indeed a tragedy, for the man radiated not only mental but physical power; every movement revealing the strength that lay in the healthy parts of his body. And yet there seemed something sinister about this latent strength, perhaps because there was a suggestion of the bird-of-prey in the sharp, aquiline nose, the thin ascetic face with its small moustache and goatee, the piercing eyes, and in the poise of the head with the longish black hair touched with grey at the temples and sweeping back from the forehead.

This was the man who sat in his invalid's chair at the desk of the president of Haghi's Bank, rapidly pencilling his directions upon the mass of papers before him, and from time to time giving curt and incisive orders over the telephone.

Lady Elinore Leslane admired Haghi's Bank more than any other building in the city, perhaps because of the practically unlimited funds which Sir Roger kept there at her disposal; and as she sat back comfortably in her mauve-coloured motor speeding toward it, her carefully rouged lips were parted in a dreamy smile, that famous smile which her many victims knew how she could use to such great advantage. She had just entered upon those years when a woman first begins to grow conscious of the fact that the sands are running rapidly through the hour-glass of time, and that life is hurrying by. This may have been the cause of the "modernistic" tendencies, which, to the great annoyance of her conservative family, she had started to develop; or her tireless pursuit of luxury and diversion may have been merely the natural reaction from the old-fashioned and saintly atmosphere in which she had been reared. At the moment, it was the knowledge that Haghi's Bank held at her call the means to satisfy some of her craving for new sensations that brought to her lips the dreamy smile.

It still lighted her face as she entered the bank, and,

at the window, the young paying-teller, falling under its spell, miscounted the notes that he handed her. Even an elderly clerk, who stepped forward to speak to her, was so disturbed that he stammered in confusion on addressing her. All of which Elinore Leslane expected as her due; she was accustomed to such reactions.

"President Haghi left word, in case Lady Leslane came into the bank, that he would like to see her a moment. He asks that her ladyship remember that he is an invalid and do him the honour of coming to his private office. He wishes to speak on a matter of business."

Elinore Leslane smiled more devastatingly than ever. She had never met the famous C. D. Haghi, for he did not go out socially, neither extending or accepting invitations on the plea of his infirmity, and she was glad to have the opportunity to see this man whose name was so great in the financial world. Invalid or no invalid, if his eyesight was unaffected there would be a new victim to the famous smile.

She followed the attendant with studied grace, and, as he announced her, entered the president's office. She found herself confronting a man seated behind a vast desk; a man who greeted her with quiet courtesy and an apology for not rising. But, for the life of her, Elinore Leslane could not have told what made her stop smiling so suddenly. Was it the effect of the room in which she found herself; a room whose austere and business-like simplicity made her feel petty and useless? Was it the woman in nurse's white who stood like an Egyptian statue behind the wheelchair, staring blankly with cold, hard eyes? Was it the studied deference with which the man in the chair asked the wife of Sir Roger Leslane to be seated, or the ominous silence that followed, pending the exit of the elderly clerk? Whatever it was, the famous smile faded from her lips, and she, the woman famed for her supreme self-possession, felt suddenly ill at ease and nervous. At the continued silence, and at the cool, appraising stare of the man, she raised her eyebrows in indignant surprise; but, to her own amazement, still waited for him to speak.

"I have some private business to discuss with you, Lady Leslane," he said at last.

Her eyes wandered questioningly to the motionless woman behind him. Haghi anticipated her.

"You need not be disturbed by Petra," he said slowly. "She is completely deaf and can hear nothing. If you wish, however, I shall dismiss her."

HAGHI

Lady Leslane shook her head. No one was more accustomed to giving orders than she, but the idea of her issuing one in this room, or to this man, struck her suddenly as impossible. "I'm sure your time is valuable," she said, trying to speak lightly. "You wanted to see me upon business, Mr. Haghi?"

Waiting for his reply, she looked at this man behind the desk with sensations which she tried to convince herself were those of mere interest, but which her thumping heart told her only too plainly were closely akin to terror. But why? Surely he should have awakened in her sympathy for his condition rather than fear. And, too, his face bore no threat, it was expressionless. But his eyes. . . . Perhaps it was his eyes . . . , or was it his silence? Why was he so silent? Why did he continue to look at her in that way instead of answering? With a flash of resentment, she started to rise.

A barely perceptible movement of the man's hand stayed her, and, leaning forward slightly, he held her with his eyes.

"Yes, on a matter of *private* business!" Her astonishment showed plainly, and a cynical smile touched the corners of his mouth. "Private business," he repeated, and continued with a quick sternness: "Lady

Leslane, within the next few days, there will be signed a treaty between . . . . shall we say between a great European nation and an Oriental power. Sir Roger Leslane will probably be present— he at least will have full knowledge concerning this event. You, his wife, will find out and report to me the exact time, date, and place, even to the room, when and where this is to take place, as well as the names of each and every person who is expected to witness the ratification."

The woman drew a deep breath of relief. She almost burst out laughing. Her self-possession had returned, and Lady Elinore Leslane rose quickly to her feet. Her voice rang out clearly: "Are you mad, Mr. Haghi?" she cried, and without deigning even to look again at the man, she turned briskly toward the door.

The voice from the wheel-chair stopped her. "You are underestimating the seriousness of the situation, my dear Lady," he said quietly. "Unless you furnish me with this information within three days, Sir Roger will, on the fourth, learn where, and in whose company his wife spends her Tuesday and Friday evenings!"

There are shocks too great to bring with them the anodyne of unconsciousness, and the woman staggered beneath just such a blow. Hence she did not faint, but remained standing, though a pitiful weakness assailed her knees, though the floor seemed to rock beneath her, and all the bells of the universe tolled in her ears. She turned back slowly. Sheer terror was in her eyes, but she fought desperately, and hopelessly, to bluff this man who sat watching her with an expressionless gaze.

"How— how— absurd!" she stammered. "How can you know anything about me?"

"In many ways, Lady Elinore," replied Haghi, with an infinitesimal shrug of his shoulders. "Perhaps, also, somewhat more than you would care to have me know." This with a deferential bow.

Elinore Leslane's eyes roved around the room in consternation. "You're lying," she gasped suddenly. "You're lying and you know it! There is nothing you can know that would give you any hold over me. I've done nothing that would put me in your power. You are merely daringly impudent. You will get your answer from Sir Roger. Sir Roger . . . ." she caught her breath with a sob, "Sir Roger will take *no one's* word against mine. He will believe nothing against me!"

"To be sure, Lady Elinore," assented the invalid quietly. "That had already occurred to me, therefore

. . . ." With a rapid movement, he took something
from his pocket and held it toward her with a gentle
smile.

It was a photograph, and she leaned forward to
see it. Her first impulse was to take hold of it, but
she did not do so. The figures in the picture were
no less inanimate than she. Nor did the man's hand
move. He held the picture up to her as if it were a
mirror— a fiendish looking-glass. It was not a work
of art. It portrayed Lady Leslane in a rather different
pose from those in which the readers of society maga-
zines and Sunday supplements were accustomed to
see her. Not surrounded by her prize dogs, nor with
a prize-winning baby-in-arms that was the envy of
half the world.

It showed an Elinore Leslane whom she herself
had never seen before— a horrible creature in horrible
surroundings, the very existence of which the wife of
Sir Roger would have denied with flaming indignation. The lens of the camera had caught this leader
of society in a position that would have been regarded
as impossibly brazen in far lower circles of humanity;
and it was little excuse that, when the picture was taken,
she knew not what she was doing. Not alcohol— that
played but a very minor part in Ah Hi's dive, but in a

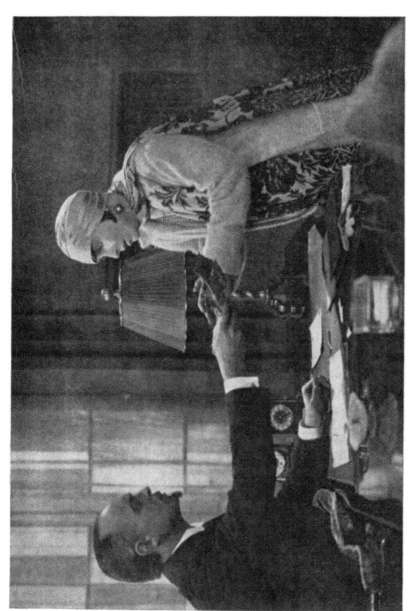

He held up the picture to her as though it were a mirror—a fiendish looking glass.

helpless stupor brought on by the insidious poison
that bubbled in Ah Hi's long stemmed pipes, entering the brain of its victims, driving men and women
mad. It had changed the exquisite wife of Sir Roger
Leslane into a degenerate beast who lay, half-wrapped
in the folds of a sleazy kimono, entwined in the arms
of a huge negro.

Strangely enough Elinore Leslane's first emotion on
seeing this picture was neither embarrassment or
shame. She was shocked out of all feelings except
those of utter amazement. When at last she managed to reach out for it, it was with the sole intent
of looking at it more closely. Curiosity stirred— the
same morbid curiosity with which a half-wit stares at
a monstrosity. Haghi let her have the photograph.
Rolling a cigarette with his stained fingers, he noted,
with the unperturbed calm of a man absolutely sure of
his case, the gamut of emotions running over her face,
which had flushed to a mottled scarlet. He watched
her with a somewhat bored patience, like a scientist at
an experiment, every phrase of which he is certain of,
having taken them all into consideration beforehand,
and who, merely as a matter of laboratory routine is
observing their actual development. He had forseen
that half-stifled moan that denoted her acceptance of

the horrible evidence. He had known that she would bite her finger nails in desperation, and could have prophesied to the moment the wild tearing to shreds of the incriminating paper and the exultant flinging of the scraps in his face. Haghi shook his head in gentle reproof.

"It is always such a disappointment, Lady Elinore," he said regretfully, "to find everyone so unoriginal. It is a pity, too, that such dramatic energy should have been wasted. You see, there still is the negative!"

From early girlhood, Elinore Leslane had had the advantages of the best of social educations. She had been carefully instructed how to meet every kind of unexpected situation; but as this education had been based on the assumption that no lady would ever find herself in a position unworthy of one of her standing, it was of little aid to her in her present predicament.

She begged and implored. She had never known that her native tongue was so rich in words of supplication— she used them all and more. But they had no effect. She did a silly thing. She flung her purse on the table— she strewed its contents of gold and notes into the rug that covered the knees of the invalid— she held out to him her check-book, sobbing: "Take everything I have— take it all!"

HAGHI

President C. D. Haghi, multi-millionaire, smiled in whimsical amusement.

Of course,— how hopeless, how stupid, to try to buy off the head of this great bank. But what else to do? She couldn't think, her brain had addled. But two things were clear: he *must* be silenced— she would never carry out his horrible orders— never, never! Dear God! What was she to do? She crept as close to the wheel-chair as she could, and smiled pleadingly into his face. She realized the failure of her effort, but the very pathos of her attempt merited a more gentle retort than she received. "Unfortunately, Lady Leslane," he said brutally, with a deliberate glance at his wrist watch, "my knowledge renders your charms somewhat unattractive to me."

Sick with shame, Elinore Leslane raised her eyes appealingly to the woman standing behind this unfeeling devil. "Madame," she begged, wringing her hands, "you are a woman, too. Won't you try to help me?"

The deaf woman continued to stare at her. As expressionless as a carven figure, she stood motionless; she scarcely breathed.

Lady Leslane collapsed despairingly into the chair from which, but a little while ago, she had risen with so much righteous indignation. For a moment, she clung to the thought of making a clean breast of everything to Sir Roger. He loved her devotedly. Perhaps she could make him understand. But no— NO! If he knew, he would keep her from opium. He would put her in some terrible institution where she would be kept under surveillance and in the torment that racked her when she missed the drug. Torment and imprisonment— and never again to bring the glossy little bead to a boil in the bowl of the long pipe— never again to float to that dreamland of poppy-fields in full bloom— wonderful fields, stretching between great glorious forests, bathed in the glow of the sun till . . . . radiant but not red . . . . almost white, with a faint rose haze shimmering over it— deepening in the distance to a mystical translucence, like the blood in one's fingers when seen against a flame. . . . No— no, she could never tell. . . . ! Torment . . . . Madness! She could kill herself. . . . . . !

"You are wasting time that doesn't belong to you, Lady Leslane," said Haghi, brusquely.

The stricken woman raised her heavy lids. The look she gave the man in the chair was not one of conscious submission, it was more a look of intense yearning. Her mind was numbed by an overpowering hunger, for the thoughts of the past moments had roused the drug-lust within her. And this was Tuesday; and last Friday Ah Hi had pretended that his supply was exhausted. Perhaps merely a ruse to enable him to raise his prices, but what did she care? She'd give him whatever price he asked. All she wanted was to dream . . . . just one dream . . . . then she would be able to think clearly.

Haghi did not ask her again whether she would obey, he gave her his orders and she nodded— he gave her his instructions, and she left.

When the door had closed behind her, the woman behind the wheel-chair *spoke,* and her eyes were filled with pain: "You grow very daring."

Haghi did not so much as turn his head. In an even voice, he said: "Send in Sonia Baranikowa. I have a new commission for her."

CHAPTER III

MOST active minded men, particularly those accustomed to irregular hours, bear in their own minds, or their subconscious minds, an alarm clock of amazing accuracy; there are but two criticisms of this mental time-piece. First,— it runs fast. Let its owner desire to awaken at eight o'clock, and this personal alarm will go off between seven and half-past. Second,— it is not a repeater. Having once performed its duty thus prematurely, it maintains a complete silence while its owner, having noted the time, sinks back for a further nap, and oversleeps.

Number 326 possessed such a personal clock. It was but about half an hour before his more trustworthy mechanical alarm would wake him that his eyes opened. For a moment or two, he lay, his hands clasped behind his head, trying to recall the events of the morning. Oh! yes. Now he had it. A chase, a hunt, a running down of big game! He sat up quickly, and laughed in the joy of it all. Perhaps an echo of the call of the wild still lingered in his soul.

He did not wait for the alarm clock to ring, but jumping out of bed, he shut it off, and stepped to the attic window. The pale sunset sky was brighter than he would have liked it to be, but the urge of the hunt was on him, and he must make a beginning.

Opening the window, he climbed out carefully, having first turned up the collar of his tattered coat and pulled down close over his eyes the brim of the disreputable hat.

There was a metal ladder to the next roof, and this he climbed, cautiously peering above the coping before stepping over. From this height he could see the huge electric sign of the Olympic Hotel blazing and blinking but a score of housetops away. As in so many misbuilt cities the rears of great buildings on the most fashionable thoroughfares opened into the slums such as that from which Number 326 was creeping like a sneak-thief.

He edged along in the shadows over the sooty roofs. An intangible danger seemed lurking behind each chimney— even the very voices of the city from below bore up to him an ominous threat. "I must be developing nerves," he muttered to himself. "It's the Chief— and that Book."

That nothing occurred on the journey over the house-tops, made him even more careful when he reached the electric sign on the top of the Olympic Hotel— by this time as black as a chimney-sweep.

He climbed down the fire-escape in the rear of the great building to the balcony outside of his bedroom, and whistled softly. Instantly the light behind the shade was extinguished, and the glass doors were opened barely enough to allow him to slip in. Franz had been on the lookout for his master. He closed the doors quickly and quietly, exclaiming, with a deep sigh of relief: "Thank the good Lord, this time is over!" That was Franz's chronic expression of greeting to his master. He was ever in a state of deep concern for the safety of this beloved dare-devil, and it was all the harder to bear because he must restrain himself to the one phrase of relief which was allowed him— "Thank the Lord."

He was particularly pleased to find his master so dirty and unkempt, for it offered him the delightful opportunity to transform this tramp, with his week's growth of beard and his filth, into Mynheer Voostenwalbert Schimmelpenninck and that would mean at least two hours safety for Number 326.

Had the devoted servant noticed, as he silently opened the doors to admit Number 326, the triple flash of the light from the building at the rear of the hotel, he might not have been so content. Perhaps, even had he been watching for these flashes, he might not have seen them, for they were carefully focussed toward the windows of another suite upon the same floor.

Number 326, disregarding entirely the effect his grimy clothes might have upon the damask upholstery, had thrown himself into a comfortable chair. Stretching out his legs, he looked up at Franz with a friendly smile that could, in itself, have accounted for the valet's devotion. "It's good to be back, Franz; and it's good to see you again. As you may see, Franz, I've missed you a bit these last few days. How about a shave and a bath?"

The faithful and simple servant, for whom only two things existed— his master, and his master's car— moved hurriedly toward the bath-room.

Down the hall, two pairs of eyes had not missed the flashes from the spotlight, because not only were they directed against the windows of their rooms, but because they were watching for them.

"Well— let's start the show," growled the voice of the owner of one pair of eyes; a pudgy, genial round-faced man, for all the world like the joke-telling travelling-salesman, and yet who was famous— that is where he was known— for his cold-blooded efficiency in murder. Come on! I want to get away. Let's go! Or shall I make it more realistic?"

His answer was the awful scream of a woman in mortal terror!

Number 326 stiffened in his chair, like an animal, startled. Somewhere, and very close, a shot had been fired. The sound came to him muffled by the thick walls, and drowned by the rush of his bath-water, but it *was* unmistakably a pistol-shot. A moment later, the corridor-door burst open, and a girl flung herself breathlessly into the room, slamming the door frantically behind her. She was trembling violently, and seemed beside herself with fear and terror. Her eyes stared wildly from a chalk-white face, and in her shaking hand she held a pistol. Franz, who had leaped from the bath-room at the slam of the door, stood gaping, rooted to the spot. Even Number 326 was, for a moment, shocked into immobility.

THE PISTOL-SHOT AT THE OLYMPIC

"For God's sake, hide me—!" she cried. "I've killed him!" She swayed, and would have fallen had not Number 326, galvanized into action, sprung to his feet and caught her in his arms. The pistol, slipping from her hand as she slumped helplessly against him, slid down his arm, and as it touched his hand he felt the barrel, still hot from its recent shot.

"I told you so— I told you so!" Franz stammered, illogically and untruthfully. This was the only other of the expressions he allowed himself when directly referring to his master, and was one he particularly favored when there was nothing else to say.

However, the considerate smile with which Number 326 usually received this comment was not forthcoming in this instance. In his surprise, he had not even heard the familiar remark.

He bent his dirty, unshaven face over that of the unconscious girl, whose head lay upon his arm, and whose warm body he held close to him. A strange and new thrill ran through him— of course it was because he had the opportunity and privilege of assisting this harassed creature who had turned to him in her hour of need. What was the warmth that crept from her to him. . . . ? God! she was beautiful! He had never noticed a woman's lips before. . . . Hers were parted . . . . invitingly . . . . If she would only open her eyes. . . . . .

His hand slipped upward until the glorious, golden crowned head lay in the crook of his arm, and the lips of Number 326, misogynist, bent slowly toward those of the unconscious woman.

A loud rap on the door— and the great eyes opened. A second rap, and louder; she struggled with the fear of the hunted, and the appeal of the helpless pleaded from the eyes he had hoped and dreaded to see. As, with a motion, he directed Franz to turn on the bath louder until its sound might well drown out the summons at the door, he, Number 326, woman-avoider, ran, in a few seconds through the whole scale of the relations between man and woman. The first knock at the door had killed the cave-man about to take his woman— the second had hurled him forward through the years to the age of chivalry; he *must* protect her— and the third, which now rapped itself to the accompaniment of the tattoo of a policeman's night-stick, yanked him to the brutal present.

She struggled in his arms, and Number 326 clapped his hand over her mouth to stifle her cry of terror. He glanced quickly at Franz, who stood in open-mouthed amazement, and the valet with a sudden re-

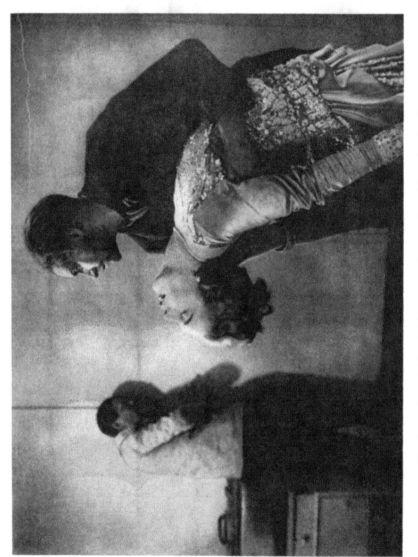

Number 326 caught her in his arms as the gun slipped from her hand.

turn to his normal, immediate comprehension of the wishes of his master, stepped silently to the door and turned the key. Outside, muffled voices were arguing excitedly.

Number 326 opened the mirrored door between his bed-room and his sitting-room. "Get in there, quick," he whispered to the trembling woman, shoving her through the doorway. He snatched the pistol from the floor. "Here, take this," he added, "and don't make a sound— don't even breathe!"

The knocking on the door became more insistent, and the tattoo of the policeman's club imperative. Number 326, rushing to the bathroom, threw on his dressing gown, rapidly lathered his face, and called loudly: "Franz! Is that someone knocking?"

The valet, quickly taking his cue, opened the door, admitting two men, who leaped into the room, each holding a drawn revolver. They brushed by the apparently dumbfounded servant, to be confronted by an obviously indignant young man, shaving-brush in hand, whose face, though covered with lather, showed his annoyance at having been interrupted in his shaving and in his bath, the water for which was running noisily in the tub, and might easily account for the ignoring of the knocking at the door. The valet, a

55

bath-sheet over one arm, stared in open-mouthed astonishment at the intruders, until his eyes fell upon the chair in which Number 326 had sat in those foul clothes; then, as if in fright, he shrank back, to drop the sheet over the too-evident stains on the chair covering, and to kick furtively beneath the chair itself the tell-tale shoes that Number 326 had left beside it.

"Well, gentlemen?" asked Number 326, in his most supercilious manner.

"We are sorry to disturb you, sir," replied the older man of the two. "I am the house detective." And indeed his profession was stamped upon him. "The officer here," indicating his companion who was in the uniform of the police, "heard the shot from outside."

"The shot?" queried Number 326. "What shot?"

"The shot that was fired on this floor not five minutes ago," continued the detective briskly. "That water running probably kept you from hearing it." He was glancing about the room as he spoke. "We're looking for a lady, sir."

"Well, what's that got to do with me?" snapped Number 326. "Is my room supposed to be full of women?"

"Hardly that, sir," replied the detective, "but we have orders to search this room for the woman."

"In Heaven's name, what woman?" exclaimed Number 326. "Why should you look here?"

"The woman, sir, who a few moments ago murdered a man on this floor, and who was seen running from his room in this direction. The maid reports that your door was not locked— in fact, that it was open, and that she thinks she saw the woman turn in here."

If the detective's eyes had been more upon the young man than busy in searching out possible hiding places in the room, he might easily have noticed the sudden tensing of the hand which gripped the flowered dressing-gown. "Murder! Murder!" The word repeated itself with the insistencey and the shock of machine-gun fire. "Murder!"

"There's a mistake somewhere," he replied sharply, maintaining his pose of irritation, "but go ahead— search as much as you like, only get it over with. I shall be late for my engagement as it is."

The two men searched the room thoroughly, and with practised skill. Number 326 leaned against the heavy wardrobe trunk that he had shoved against the mirrored door. He still held his shaving-brush in one hand, while the other clutched the dressing-gown that concealed the filthy tramp clothes. He blessed the rapidly drying lather for hiding the pallor of his face; and he kept upon his lips a tolerant smile, as he watched the two men. "What the devil is the matter with me?" he asked himself indignantly, as he felt the tremor that ran through him.

The detective stepped out upon the balcony, and through the door floated a fragment of dance music. Number 326 imagined he could hear the thumping of the frightened heart and the stifled sobs of the girl, in fear of her life, behind the mirrored door. "Don't you be afraid," he found himself thinking, as if speaking to her. "Don't be afraid— I'll see you safely through this." But murder! the word echoed in his brain. Murder! It couldn't be! That girl was incapable of such a crime. And yet there had been a shot— and she had carried a pistol— and it had been still warm— There must be some explanation, a dream — a nightmare? He closed his eyes for a moment in his perplexity, and the beauty of her face, and the glory of those pleading eyes seemed glowing against his eyelids.

He opened them with a start at the sound of the detective's voice apologizing for the unfortunate annoyance. The latter was about to go, when he hesitated. His glance had fallen on the wardrobe trunk.

"Beg pardon, sir," he said gravely. "We'd like to know what's back of that."

Number 326 felt a sudden constriction at this heart, and out of the corner of his eye he saw Franz set himself for battle. But he answered calmly enough: "Go ahead," and stepped aside.

The policeman dragged the trunk to one side, exposing the mirrored door. He tried the knob, and Number 326 grew tense, ready to spring. The door was locked from the other side! "Oh," said the officer, "belongs to the next suite. Once again we apologize for troubling you."

Number 326 bowed in a somewhat bored fashion, and condescended to accept graciously their expressions of regret. They offered to replace the trunk, but Number 326 assured them that his valet was quite capable of doing that, and motioned Franz to show them out.

No sooner had the door closed behind them, Franz again carefully locking it, than Number 326 hastily wiping his lathered face with his hands, rushed to the mirrored door, only to step back again in chagrined embarrassment at his own reflection.

"Good God," he ejaculated, "did she see me like this?" And, indeed, the unkempt, matted hair, the

59

smeary, unshaven face, the foul odorous rags— all begrimed with soot and mould— made no charming picture. "The devil!" he exclaimed again.

Years of experience had taught Franz to anticipate his master's wishes, and now, into the bathroom he plunged without a word. In less than ten minutes, the valet smiled, as Number 326 again walked to the mirror, and this time contemplated his reflection with obvious satisfaction.

In reply to the whispered question as he knocked on the door, Number 326 answered softly: "It's me."

The key turned slowly in the lock, and Number 326 opened the door that separated him from the girl. She was half-crouching, close behind the door, trembling like a frightened, cornered fawn, breathing in short, quick gasps, her eyes wide with terror. But, when she looked at this exceedingly well-groomed young man, clean-shaven and handsome, and the realization came to her that he and the filthy tramp were one and the same, the look of fear in her eyes gave way to one of unbelieving amazement, and admiration.

For a long moment they stood gazing at each other, and Number 326 was conscious of a new feeling that surged within him,— a great longing that poured forth toward this girl, to whose pallid face the colour suddenly rushed. For a long moment they stood, and neither could have said how long; and, then, with a quick, nervous laugh: "It can't be possible," she exclaimed.

"But it is," he replied, with a slight shake of his head, as if to clear it. "And I hope you like the change," he added.

"It's wonderful. I never should have recognized you." She was speaking hurriedly, as if just to say something, it hardly mattered what. "Why you're positively good-looking, and— how strange!— you're the image of my own brother, my own dear brother whom I loved more than anything on earth. . . . Only you're a bit fairer than he, and less serious— but you're nothing but a boy, and. . . ." she broke off suddenly, beneath his steady gaze.

"I am sorry you think that," said he seriously, "for, at this moment, I do not feel youthful— I have just acquired the wisdom of all the ages." The girl's hands were clasped together, and he did not notice their quick tensing, as, relaxing again to a smile, he continued: "But, if I am nothing but a boy— what then are you?"

"Oh! I don't know *what* I am," she cried, "I don't ever know myself— Nobody knows— nobody— I'll be whatever you want me to be. . . ." and with an embarrassed realization of what she was saying, turned her head quickly from him. Her eyes fell upon the table, where, quite forgotten, lay the ugly, steel-blue automatic.

A choking sob arose in her throat, and she raised an agonized face to Number 326, through whose mind rang the horrid echo of that sinister word: "Murder!"

Angrily, he hurled the very thought from him, and stepped, with out-stretched arms, toward this lovely thing with the pleading violet eyes and shimmering golden hair. But she drew back from him. Her eyes were filling with tears, and before he had time to speak, she had broke into an uncontrollable spasm of weeping. These were not tears of relief, nor of fear, but seemed to burst from a heart that was breaking in grief. He could not understand. Why had she turned away from him so violently? Her vehemence, as she threw herself against the door, and beat it wildly with her fists, frightened him. He did not know what to do.

"Dear," he said at last, very gently, "dear," he did not know what else to call her, and it was astonishing how easily the word slipped from his lips, "you mustn't— what's the trouble? You must tell me— I can help you. You *must* trust me."

THE PISTOL-SHOT AT THE OLYMPIC

She turned her head at his words, and Number 326 made the unusual discovery that a woman can weep and still remain lovely to look upon. She hesitated for a moment, and then, controlling herself with a visible effort, and wringing the words from her lips with difficulty, she stammered: "I had an engagement to meet— him— here, at the hotel. We were to— discuss the possibility of a— South American contract— Rio— He tried to— he wanted— to— I was petrified— I didn't know what to do— the first thing I knew, I had the gun in my hand, and I had— shot him!" She gasped in horror as she uttered the last words.

Number 326 took her twitching cold hands in his. At first she struggled to release herself, and avoided his eyes, cowering like an animal caught in a trap; but, though neither of them afterward could remember just what he had said, his gentle voice calmed her; gradually her tears ceased and the racking sobs subsided. She lifted her face to his, a face so filled with pathos and misery and something more than gratitude, that the man lapsed into quick silence.

She stared at him as if to burn his picture forever in her memory. She smiled wanly— a pitiful attempt at a smile— and then closed her eyes— only to reopen them as if to convince herself of the reality of the situation, and to make sure that her memory would not play her false. Once again she looked up at Number 326 as though to make certain that not a single detail of that frank countenance had escaped her notice. "I trust you with my whole heart and soul," she cried. "I shall never forget you!"

Number 326 felt his heart leap within him, but restrained himself: "Let me have Franz, my chauffeur, take you to his mother's," he suggested, in as calm a voice as he could muster. "It's a simple little place, and you'll be safe there— they are the sort who don't ask questions about my affairs. Will you go?"

She nodded, as if afraid to speak.

"She is still on the verge of tears," thought the man.

He put his arms about her and led her toward a chair. "Excuse me just one moment while I tell Franz what to do. I'll be right back."

As he turned to go, she seized him quickly by the shoulders. "You beautiful, clean boy," she cried fiercely, "how could anyone not trust you— you're more than wonderful— you're good!" and with a quick movement she pulled his face down to hers, kissed him full on the lips and flung herself into the chair, burying her head in the cushions.

Paralyzed with amazement and delight, he stood eagerly leaning toward her, and then rushed into the bedroom. In his exhilaration, he failed utterly to notice Franz's curious expression, or that the latter tried to interrupt him several times as he gave his instructions. At last, the valet was able to break through the barrage of excited words.

"But, sir," he blurted out, "the man is not dead at all!"

"What?" gasped his master.

"It was all a mistake," replied Franz. "She didn't even hit him— the bullet lodged in a brief-case. The fellow's still scared to death, but he won't make any fuss, not if he knows which side his bread is buttered on. He's already asked the police and the management to hush up the matter, and the management has already told him to get out and stay out."

A great load lifted from his mind, Number 326 flung open the door of the drawing-room: "Dear," he cried, "dear one. . . . . !"

The room was empty!

The chair, its cushions still bearing the imprint of her beautiful body, was vacant; the tag on the key in the door through which she had fled was still swinging to and fro in the lock; the ink was not yet dry on the note that was lying on the table where a few moments before the pistol had rested.

The room reeled— his heart seemed to stop in its beat— a numbness crept through him— he was dazed. "When he breaks, he is going to break badly," Chief Jason had thought of him. Had the Chief been present he would have viewed the truth of his prophecy.

Beside himself, Number 326 snatched the note from the table:

"It will be far better for you if we never meet again."

He tore to the door to rush out and to follow her, but halted at the threshold. At the very same moment, a man had opened the door across the hall. This man, standing with one hand on the knob, evidently an Oriental, whose long jet-black hair, parted in the middle, gave to his face almost the appearance of a kindly old lady, wore heavy-rimmed spectacles through which peered a pair of dark and unfathomable eyes. It was the piercing look of these, the slight negative shake of the head, and the barely perceptible smile that hovered about the thin lips, that held Number 326 within his doorway. The Oriental bowed slightly, and very slowly. The European returned the salutation mechanically, then with a strange acceptance of this silent, and mysterious warning, stepped back, and closed his door.

He remained standing in the centre of that indescribably deserted room. Like a man who has been stabbed, he stood there— hurt to the core, and fearfully shocked.

Franz watched his master in distressed wonderment. Never had he seen Number 326 dazed and bewildered. He was at a loss; neither of his two set remarks— "Thank the Lord that's over" or "I told you so"— seemed appropriate. One comment would not be true, and the other certainly would not be welcome. Hence, he tip-toed to the other room, closed the door silently, sank into a chair, shaking his head dejectedly, and cursed softly to himself.

Number 326 remained motionless, staring blankly at nothing, experiencing for the first time the mystical emptiness of a room from which a fragrance, a smile, a voice had gone, leaving behind nothing save a terrible yearning for them. . . . . .

"When he breaks, he will break badly!"

CHAPTER IV

THE SPIDER IN HIS WEB

"You have been crying, and apparently with great realism," mocked Haghi in his quiet voice. "You must have played your part with real dramatic fervour, my dear Sonia."

Sonia Baranikowa did not answer. She winced under the sneering tone as under the flick of a lash, but did not summon the courage to show openly the anger she felt. Haghi, watching her keenly, continued mechanically to roll one of his ever-present cigarettes. Petra, the nurse, stood immobile, behind his chair, her long lashes throwing dark shadows on her waxen face. The silence was intense; the monotonous ticking of the electric clock on the desk became nerve-wracking, and even the tread of the sentinels in the hall-way beyond the almost sound-proof double door seemed loud.

This was not the office of President C. D. Haghi, of

68

Haghi's Bank, for plainly furnished as that was it seemed luxurious in comparison to this austere room, which, with its cold stone walls, unrelieved by any window looked more like a great prison cell. A vast desk, at one side of which bent a hooded chute that shot forth a constant stream of papers before the sombre figure in the invalid chair, and at the other a similar chute into which he dropped his briefly pencilled orders, and two chairs were all that this room contained. No more was needed, for few indeed ever saw the inside of it, and most who were favoured by admittance to this strange sanctum remained standing deferentially.

Concealed behind the imposing structure of Haghi's Bank and separated from it by walls of the heaviest vault construction, pierced only by one hidden passage, was a great building, whose very presence was unsuspected by the city authorities. Camouflaged on the street frontage by offices and stores, it covered a vast area; it was indeed a city within a city, an amazing net-work of secret passages, a veritable maze of courts, of hidden chambers, of exits and entrances, of cells and rooms equipped with countless sending and receiving apparatus. For this was the Headquarters of a great secret organization, the hiding place of a marvellously developed and complicated spy system, the strong-hold and the refuge of its members. No precautions for its defence had been overlooked. Its walls were impenetrable, and night and day by each of the exits and entrances paced two guards, in full battle equipment, including hand grenades and gas masks. For, the release of one lever, would in a few seconds, flood the whole interior of the vast structure with poison gas. The red button, covered against accidental pressure by the nickel plate at the right side of the vast desk in the bare blind-walled stone room, alone controlled that lever; for this room was the very centre of the web, and the low-voiced cripple in the invalid chair the spider who had spun it, and who received there each tiny quiver of the countless radiating threads; no longer President C. D. Haghi, famous financier, but Haghi, the Chief— the Master Mind whose orders every member of his vicious brotherhood obeyed without question and to the letter.

Sonia Baranikowa paced up and down with nervous, aimless footsteps. She did not realize how clearly she showed herself to be struggling to accept a hopeless situation. Her shimmering silver evening gown, her pale features under the glistening gold of her hair stood out in vivid contrast to that threatening and repelling chamber.

THE SPIDER IN HIS WEB

Haghi waited in calculated silence for the girl to speak first. He knew that much of his success in handling people could be attributed to just that— they would always speak when the strain became unbearable. He could see even now that Sonia was breaking under that wordless tension; and she knew it. Struggle as best she might against the terrible will of that suave, relentless man, who sat in his wheel chair motionless except for his eyes which never left his face, she knew she could not hold out against him long. Yet she *must* try.

"Use any one else, Haghi," she burst out at last.

"Let some one else handle this job— only leave me out of it. I won't have anything more to do with it."

Haghi raised his eye-brows questioningly.

"And if not, why not?"

Sonia did not answer; she stared over the head of the man at the blank stone wall, and bit her lips. "Why did I say anything?" she asked herself remorsefully. "Now he'll pry into my very soul and find out everything— he'll read my thoughts like a book— he'll tear out my heart, just as I've found that I have one."

"And if not, why not," repeated Haghi.

There was no escaping; she was trapped. She knew his powers, and her impotence. She turned her head away in anguish.

71

"I simply don't want to be your agent in this case.
I don't want to work against this man any more."

She felt his eyes penetrate her brain like X-rays.

"And if not, why not?" he purred, for the third
time.

She bowed her head: "Because— because he— he
reminds me so much of my brother, Sacha," she lied,
and knew that he did not believe her.

"What a marvellous memory you have, my dear,"
observed Haghi, suavely, leaning back in his chair.
"Were you not but a child when your brother died?
Let's see. . . . If my own memory doesn't play me
false, he died, didn't he, together with your father, because he had been denounced to the Ochrana. And they
were executed, were they not, because they believed in
the new dawn of Freedom? And wasn't it just that,
that drove you to us; like us, sick with hatred for the
present order of things, sick with hatred for the men
in power and their unjust laws? Wasn't it that hatred
.that has made you my best and most zealous worker—
that fired you with enthusiasm which made you keener
and more relentless than any other except myself?
Why, my dear Sonia, the very fact that you have been
reminded of your brother ought to make you even
more eager to fight this government spy, help us dis-

pose of him— as with the others— or perhaps—" he stopped to roll another cigarette, and to question the girl with a cynical, insinuating smile— "win him over to our side."

"Never— never!" gasped the girl, in sudden horror. "That would be impossible!"

"Why?" asked Haghi calmly. "It may easily be the best way to handle this case. Your very abrupt departure from his rooms," the girl's eyes opened wide in her surprise at this evidence of his knowledge, "left your little one-act comedy hanging in mid-air. Your visit was, also, a distressing failure: a piece of useless blotting paper, a few worthless letters. This Number 326 is Miles Jason's largest trump, too dangerous to leave in the hand of my opponent. Either I must manipulate the cards so as to get it myself, or—" and he leaned forward and spoke with sinister meaning, "the *whole* hand must be destroyed, *Trump* and all!

"I can use a man of his calibre," continued Haghi, after a pause. "I have wanted him for some time, but until now have found no way of getting him. He is not a man to fear threats, nor can he be bought— with money! But now, it comes to me that very probably he might be skillfully enticed to a point from which it would be difficult for him to turn back, and then lured even further until he joins our forces of his own accord. And who, I ask yourself, and who, my dear, could— er— influence a young man better than the beautiful Sonia Baranikowa, my most alluring, my most charming and most irresistible spy?"

He had spoken softly and deliberately, weighing each word carefully, yet each word stung the girl like so much merciless, driving sleet. She shivered, frozen to the spot, her eyes raised in a fixed glassy stare.

"Sit down," ordered Haghi, and turning to the woman behind him he made some motions with his fingers.

Sonia obeyed mechanically. Petra's clammy hands placed before her a sheet of writing paper and a fountain pen.

"Write as follows," commanded Haghi:

"My Dear Friend:"

The pen moved automatically.

"I feel that I owe you an explanation. I wish very much for the opportunity to give it to you in person.—"

Sonia threw down the pen violently, and rose to her feet.

"I will not write this letter, Haghi," she stated firmly. "You can do what you want with me, but I won't write another word!"

THE SPIDER IN HIS WEB

The man did not shift his imperturbable eyes from her face. She was ghastly white, and trembled at her own temerity, yet she met his look with one of rebellion and indignation. Without releasing her from his hypnotic stare, Haghi proceeded very deliberately to roll another cigarette. Petra lighted it for him. He puffed away silently for several tense moments.

"Sonia," and beneath the gentle voice lay a terrible menace. "Sonia, even you may go too far some day. Now, omit the phantasy about your brother and the wonderful resemblance, and tell me why."

"Because," she flung back heatedly, "never in my whole life have I despised anything or anyone as I despised and hated myself and you to-night, when your accomplice and I acted that vile farce at the Olympic! Oh yes, yes, I know," she exclaimed in answer to his quizzical look, "he was my accomplice as well— and I his— and I hate myself the more for it.

"But Haghi, I am not trying to break with you— I'm not asking anything except that you won't force me to trick shamefully this man, who, without hesitating an instant because of the possible consequences to himself, came to my rescue because he thought I needed his protection and help."

75

"A matter of conscience, then, and pity, and sympathy," asked Haghi, in mock surprise. "But, again, why? For, if I remember correctly, it was relying on this very sense of chivalry— this heroic folly, that a beautiful woman can almost invariably awaken in a young man— though we were doubtful in this case— upon which we based our whole plan. And, what is more, it comes to me very distinctly that the whole scheme, including the faked murder, had its conception in that clever head of yours. Isn't that correct, Sonia?"

"Yes," muttered the girl, as if the admission choked her.

"And now, without any new developments entering the case, with the chivalrous young man swallowing the bait as we had hoped, and counted on his doing— you must have acted your part splendidly, Sonia!— you suddenly refuse to go on playing that part. Why?"

Sonia saw his eyes turn to jade, and when he continued the soft mocking tone had roughened to a brute harshness:

"I can tell you why, you little fool! Do you think I don't know what went on in those rooms? Do you believe you can hood-wink Haghi? Within two minutes after you saw him, as himself, not as the tramp, you were desperately in love with him, as he, the fool also, for the first time, was with you. That is what has given you the rashness to attempt to question my orders. If you were not more valuable to me alive, you would not be able to hear me now. If I did not want this man, he, too, would be out of the way. Sonia Baranikowa, you are fortunate to have the opportunity to save your lover's life and your own. You are the only one who has the power."

For a moment, the girl, stunned almost beyond consciousness, stood rigid and motionless; then, with a stifled moan, she fell limply into her chair. The stony eyes of the attendant followed her, and seemed to soften in pity, but the man remained expressionless, quietly rolling another cigarette.

Again, the silence was broken only by the ticking of the clock, and the muffled sound of the sentries' tread.

"Shall we continue the letter?" asked Haghi, at last, his voice once more caressingly gentle. "Do you remember what I had told you to write?"

Sonia slowly raised her head, and nodded despairingly.

"Then, write it, my dear."

She did as she was told.

Haghi continued the dictation:

"Do come tomorrow afternoon, and have a glass of real Russian tea, at four o'clock— with the woman you rescued."

"Sign yourself with your initials only. Address the letter to 'Apartment 119-120, The Olympic', and write your own address on the flap of the envelope. The rest I leave to you.

"Now one more thing. How far have you gotten with Jellusic?"

The girl replied wearily: "He's ready."

"Good," said Haghi. "That matter must be closed at once; he's being watched. They've tried to find out under what cipher he is getting his mail at the General Delivery."

"He's not the only one who is being watched," remarked the girl, in a dull voice.

Haghi jerked up his head.

"What do you mean by that?" he snapped. "Who else?"

"I found a Japanese peddler at my door, when I got home last night," replied Sonia, listlessly. "He pretended to be selling curios, but I believe that he had been listening at the keyhole. There wasn't anything wrong with the lock, but it looked greasy, as if wax had been used for an impression. This afternoon while I was waiting for Jellusic— he had gone to get the plans at the post-office— I noticed a man sitting in an open-air café next door, a man who had hidden his face in a Japanese newspaper."

"Hmm!" muttered Haghi. Then, curtly: "Why haven't you told me this before?" His lips formed into a hard thin line.

"You have given me other things to think about," said Sonia. "I had forgotten about it until now."

Haghi coughed dryly. "It displeases me to have my assistants forget things. . . . . ."

The girl remained silent.

"Is that understood, Sonia?"

"Quite."

"Good. I trust you will regard it as a privilege that I take the trouble to remind you. As you know. . . . . ."

"I have already told you that I understand you, Haghi," interrupted the girl calmly. It was as if the very worst had happened, and she had nothing more to fear. "Have you any further instructions for me?"

He shot an angry look at her, considered for a moment, and replied: "Yes. As far as Jellusic is concerned, I am ready to pay him; but I must have the plans by tomorrow night, and he must cross the frontier immediately. Arrange your plans so that you

will be at the post-office entrance between 9:15 and
9:30 P.M. Morrier will be waiting for you. He will
give you further instructions. Is that clear?"

"Quite."

"Then, good-night, my dear Sonia," and as an after-
thought, he added, with a wry smile, "pleasant dreams
to you."

She flashed a bitter glance at him, and dragged herself wearily toward the door, which, as Haghi moved
a lever beside his desk, opened soundlessly to let her out.

Sonia walked mechanically toward the nearest exit,
mechanically returning the guard's salute, and mechanically giving him the pass-word. Her thoughts were
too busy for her to notice her surroundings. What
could she do? She must save him— this man, who,
in but a few minutes, had become more to her than
her life. That, she would gladly have sacrificed, but
she must remain living to protect him, and to protect
him she must trick him and shamelessly lure him to
dishonour!

She could not betray Haghi. Terrible, relentless as
he was— ruthless and ghastly as were his methods and
actions— he was driving with irresistible force toward
his end— the end which was her ideal: the destruction
of injustice, the establishment of the brotherhood of

man— and the end would justify his means, horrible as they often were.

Perhaps she could persuade Him to abandon his work— but in an instant she realized the impossibility of this; those that love truly quickly know the souls of their lovers.

She gave the guard at the secret exit an absent-minded but at the same time such a bewildering smile that he quite forgot to ask her for the password. He silently pushed back the heavy metal door that opened into the cellar of a fruit-store, and, giving her the usual salute, permitted her to pass. She groped her way through the dark to the stairs leading up to the back of the store, climbed these slowly, and, still wrapped in her thoughts, made her way to the street.

She decided not to take a taxi— a walk would be rather refreshing. Through the sleeping city, between poverty-stricken houses which seemed to glower at her threateningly, as if they resented her being abroad at that hour, she walked slowly— thinking— thinking.

And with the fresh air came clarity of reason, and courage, and with courage came decision. She would stay, and she would fight! She would fight Haghi to the bitter end on this one point, and fight him as he himself had taught her. What though this cripple issued from his wheel chair orders that were more far reaching than those from a throne— what though his power seemed almost infinite— something within her flushed her face with the enthusiasm of a Crusader, something cried aloud, "fight, for God is with you!"

She squared her shoulders, and in the action dropped from them the load of hopeless depression. She drew a full, deep breath, gloriously conscious of her young strength and energy. The steeple clocks chimed the hour of four.

"Only twelve hours to wait," she thought happily. "He surely will come. I must get my sleep." And laughing in her new-found joy she hurried on.

She became conscious of rapid footsteps behind her. They grew closer, until she broke into a run. Then she knew she was being followed,— for she could hear her pursuer following her with the light tread of a trained athlete and runner. She wheeled sharply. Her angry eyes met those of the man at her heels. Sturdy, well-built as he was there was a suggestion of slinking about him, and a certain rat-like quality in his expression— Morrier. Morrier, Haghi's spy upon his spies— Morrier, with his ever-merry rogue's face, whose tiny black moustache was forever drawn from over his sharp white teeth in an ingratiating smile.

"What is the meaning of this?" snapped Sonia, angrily.

Morrier swept his cap from his head. His smile broadened. No one had ever seen that smile completely leave his face, not even when he stood in the shadow of the gallows he had so richly deserved, and from which Haghi's men had snatched him. That accounted for his abject devotion to his master— a scoundrel, faithful to a fiend he believed a god.

"Phew! Sonia," he exclaimed, "you certainly know how to cover ground. I'm all out of wind." He laughed again in sincere admiration, his white teeth flashing in his sallow face.

"What do you mean, following me like this, Morrier?" demanded the girl.

Morrier dropped one eye-lid in a knowing wink. "The Chief," he replied, "thought that perhaps you might not be quite *safe!*" He threw back his head in merry laughter.

Sonia could not mistake the double meaning. Her face grew suddenly weary, and her eyes lost the light that had filled them but a few moments before.

"Oh! leave me and get to bed, Morrier," she re-

83

torted. "You can tell the Chief that I am quite safe."
She turned her back upon him abruptly, and went on; but was fully conscious, nevertheless, of the shadow that followed her, always close enough to watch her— a relentless shadow that she would not be able to lose; for well she knew the fanatical devotion of this man behind her to the master who had plucked him from between the fingers of Death. Haghi's own watchfulness was easy to elude, for he never watched except through the countless peep-holes and "periscopes" that covered every room in his stronghold, each periscope flashing its image on the screen set before his desk. But Morrier! Had Haghi assigned him to watch her, she could never escape. She, herself, had profited too often by his tireless vigilance. And Morrier gauged people solely on their value to his master. What was she worth to Haghi now? Haghi, himself, seemed in doubt— or why Morrier on her heels— and she herself could not answer the question. But, Morrier seemed to know, and he adjusted his actions accordingly.

CHAPTER V

THE RUSSIAN TEA

At three and one-half minutes before four o'clock, there drew up before the door of the address that Sonia Baranikowa had written on the flap of the enforced note to Number 326 a handsome car, on the driver's seat of which sat a sullen-faced chauffeur. The occupant of the tonneau leaped out.

"I don't know how long I shall be, Franz. Wait here."

"But your Excel—"

"Franz!" snapped the passenger.

The driver gulped the rest of the word, but continued: "Master, take your revolver, at least. You don't know. . . . . ."

"It would spoil the fit of my coat, you old chump," replied the other. "And Franz, didn't you really see her? What have I to be afraid of here?"

Neither of Franz's stock remarks could apply to

85

that question, but he earnestly looked forward to the moment when he could breathe to himself, at least, "Thank the Lord, that's over!"

Number 326 ran joyfully up the steps to the door. In his eagerness he did not notice Franz steal up behind him. The door was opened by a stolid, middle-aged maid, at whom Number 326 looked with sudden attention. Having given his card, he stepped inside, and as the door closed behind him, neither he nor the maid saw Franz slip in the light but stiff card that prevented the latch from catching.

"Well, now," remarked this strategist, "if he can't get out, I can get in." There were other devoted servants beside Morrier.

The little salon into which Number 326 was ushered seemed to him less of a room than a sanctuary; it was only softly visible, like an old chapel. The air was redolent of roses. He hesitated a moment on the threshold, drinking in the soft beauty, and sensing the memories from which it had been created— or resurrected. It spoke in gentle pathos, and of the yearning of a lonely exile, of one who had tried to rebuild the shattered fragments of a beloved past.

Sonia, who had descended silently, watched him through an opening in the portieres. Had she needed more, it was there, this evident understanding— and her heart throbbed in her breast. In her arms, she carried the roses he had sent. She wondered if there were a significance in the fact that they were all in bud. He had sent a note with them, also a newspaper clipping, in a style which she knew only too well— Haghi, who had disposed of the hotel episode with a few ironical phrases. Number 326 had pencilled on the margin of the clipping: "Then those tears were ordained just to bring you closer to me."

Sonia shamelessly continued to spy on her guest. She marvelled at the freshness of him, the clean wholesomeness of his face, which, despite his years in a service which brings of necessity disillusion in humanity, showed no sign or mark of it. She noticed with a happy poignance the reverence with which he was looking at her small possessions— the tenderness with which he studied the miniatures of her dead father and brother. She understood— he was trying to know her better through her personal belongings and private treasures.

"Oh! I love you," she whispered to herself. "I love you, you nameless boy, and as long as I live he shall not harm you."

She threw aside the portieres and entered the room.

The young man swung about sharply, stepped quickly toward her, and told her with his lips his thanks for her invitation, and with his eyes what it meant to him.

Convention and its habits, and shyness, held them apart. Convention was strong enough to make them yield to the banality of shaking hands— shyness on the part of each alone prevented the close embrace that was the proper greeting between them. And yet the very handclasp was a profession of their love.

The girl was the first to break the spell, forcing back the tears that the adoration from his eyes brought to her own. "I am so glad you could come," she murmured politely, and berated herself for her cowardice.

"I am very glad to be here," replied Number 326, damning himself that he had lacked the courage to take her in his arms. But she had been formal, and so must he be. And, then, with an inspiration: "But I have been remiss." He reached for her hand, and bowing low over it he pressed it fervently with his hot lips.

She barely restrained her desire to fold him in her other arm and to hold him close to her. The motion was on its way, when the horrid knowledge of her situation held her back. Very gently, reluctantly, she withdrew her hand.

"And aren't you going even to ask me who I am," she said abruptly, smiling through the unshed tears she prayed he did not see. "My name is Sonia— Sonia Nikolovena Baranikowa. And now, what is yours?" She held her breath, and forced herself to smile, for she knew that he could not answer truthfully.

"What's in a name?" he quoted with a slight shrug. "Don't laugh at me, Sonia Nikolovena, but I haven't any name! Of course, I use one but it is assumed, not real. Call me anything you like, but don't make me tell you a lie."

"I won't— and thank you— my dear." She paused, her thoughts wandering in apparent distress, then, pulling herself together with a visible effort, she began to talk rapidly, and with an artificial and forced composure. "Please sit down. Sit here on the divan, and we'll have the tea I promised you. I'm so glad you like my little room. I can see true appreciation reflected in your eyes— it *is* charming, isn't it? But you'll have to wait until some other time before I can tell you really what it means to me. Then you'll be able to understand many things that could only puzzle you to-day. Please don't smile at my talkativeness, but let me go on chattering. Ordinarily I've either got to keep quiet, or else say things that I'd rather not say.

that's part of my job— my profession demands it. Do you like your tea strong?"

The young man facing her was so lost in admiring her loveliness that he but half heard. Aroused from his reverie, he nodded his head hastily, and, seeing her startled look, coloured in embarrassment. What had she asked? Oh! the tea— thanks, he wouldn't take any.

The courage to fight which had come to the girl the night before seemed to be deserting her. A nausea of fear swept over her as she looked upon this stranger who had become the whole world, and realized the future that lay ahead of them both.

Her restless hands again offered him tea, cognac, sugar, lemon, cream, in nervous tension. He merely shook his head to all of them, and continued to gaze at her in rapt adoration, his eyes pleading. At last she knew the futility of further pretense. She pushed aside the tea-tray, and held out both her hands. He took them gently in his own and reverently pressed his lips to them. "Beloved," he asked, raising his head, "do I have to tell you in words?"

She did not know that she had moved— she only felt her heart beating frantically— or was it his heart

"Do trust me," he begged.　"Let me help you."

she felt throbbing against her own— his eager kisses
on her warm, responsive lips.

"Dearest, dearest Galahad," she half sobbed, "I've
known you all my life......"

The slanting rays of the setting sun flooded the
room, suffusing it with amber light, as if in benediction; and, falling on an ancient jewel-studded chalice,
fired the gems until they gleamed with a ruby radi-
ance— a veritable Grail .... sunset .... and twilight .... and gradually dusk in the little room......

The sudden flash of a street-lantern bursting into
light, and the shrill cry of a newsboy calling the evening papers, broke the spell that had held the man and
the girl entranced, oblivious to the passing of time, lost
to the world in their rapture.

They stared at each other in startled wonder. He
released her from his embrace, as they both laughed
happily in sweet embarrassment, only to yield immediately to the impulse to take her in his arms again.

"I'm stealing these precious hours," thought the man.

"I'm stealing," thought the girl, "I'm stealing these
precious hours."

"Let me have this one evening with you," whispered
the man. "Sonia dearest, I don't know what is to happen to me. I can't tell when I shall be able to see you

again. I know only one thing certainly— that I love you! Give me to-night! Sonia, you aren't listening to me!"

Not listening to him— Oh, God! He did not know what was to happen to him! Did she?

"Of course I am listening. I am only dizzy with happiness, dear boy," she lied. (What is to become of us, what is to become of us?) "And there is another thing which is certain: I love you more than my life."

The man closed his eyes for a second, and passed his hand across his forehead as if to brush away some disturbing thought. He rose to his feet and bent over the girl whose face was raised to his in infinite tenderness.

"I *must* go now, beloved," he said hurriedly. "I'll be back for you at nine o'clock. We'll have dinner at Danielli's, yes? Does that suit you?"

"I'll wear my loveliest frock in your honor," promised the girl, "and look my very best so that I shall not shame the handsomest and most wonderful escort a woman ever had."

He smothered her adoring enthusiasm in a passionate embrace, released her with an effort, and rushed toward the door. But half way, he turned as if she had called him. She stretched out her arms, and, leaping back, he held her close, covering her lips, her throat, her closed eyes with burning kisses.

"Make me go— send me away, dear, oh! my very dear," he murmured. "Please, please send me off, send me on my way."

She tore herself reluctantly from his arm, and, bracing her hands against his breast, pushed him back.

"On your way, then!" she gasped breathlessly, tossing back the golden crown of her hair with an exultant laugh. "Along with you, beloved bandit, who has robbed me of my heart and my love."

His second effort to reach the door was successful, but, having opened it, he shut it again quietly, and hesitated with his hand on the knob. A troubled shadow darkened his face.

"Dearest one," he said seriously, "do you know anything about your maid? Do you know that she has served a sentence in prison?"

Sonia's heart stood still— the maid was a trusted member of the Organization. "Oh! yes," she answered quickly, "she is with me on probation. Don't worry, dear, she will not murder me in my sleep."

Part of the shadow lifted, but he continued: "If—if apparently unexplainable things happen— I cannot say any more, dear, even to you— please believe in me, and perhaps— forgive me. At nine o'clock, then." He stepped quickly through the doorway and was gone.

Not until then did Sonia remember that not a word had been said about her mysterious running away from his rooms.

For a long time the girl stood staring at the closed door. Unexplainable things! Would *he* believe— would *he* forgive? He had *not* asked about yesterday— perhaps he would forgive? A pathetically hopeful smile crept to her lips.

Through the half-open window came the rumble of distant thunder.

CHAPTER VI

THE DEVIL DRIVES

DANIELLI'S was a most exclusive establishment, and even more distinguished than its clientele, was its remarkable personnel.

It was a gathering-place for fallen nobility; a quiet backwater where had been swept by the raging torrent of the war years the broken branches of great family trees.

The Chef had been the greatest epicure in European royalty. His present achievements were far more commendable than those for which he had been noted when he sat upon his throne. His gravies outdid Larne's— his lobsters put Prunier to shame. Both *gourmand* and *gourmet* travelled miles to smack their lips over "Truffel à la Danielli"; and many a wealthy fool paid a small fortune for the privilege of seeing His Majesty reign in his kitchen, administering the affairs of his culinary domain.

The doors of the cars which drew up in the charming driveway were opened by a former flying Ace, whose own propeller had deprived him of one arm. He spent his mornings at an agricultural school, his afternoons learning to type with one hand, and his evenings receiving nonchalantly the generous tips of Danielli's patrons, and the languishing looks of lovely ladies.

The Doorman, resplendent in a uniform far more ornate than that of his previous exalted rank, had been an Admiral in the Imperial Navy— with a Grand Duchess for a wife. All that was left of that past grandeur were his flowing white beard, and his memories of the Grand Duchess, who had disappeared during the revolution which had made him a proscribed fugitive. It was his earnest hope, and most fervent daily prayer, that she would not suddenly bob up again and spoil the peaceful contentment of his days.

Danielli's manager was an ex-diplomat, a man with the most exquisite manners, and the head-waiter a deposed Arch-Duke, whose dignity and evident discretion were so admirable that no one ever ventured to question his addition of a check. In consequence his apartment, his car, and his horses were all remarkably fine.

THE DEVIL DRIVES

And yet it was the orchestra which was famous on two continents. Its leader was the son of a multimillionaire, who, fed up with spending his father's millions had joined the gypsy band, and who supported himself by his violin. When he stepped forward to play, the silence was immediate, and as he drew his bow across the strings, every woman within hearing could be counted upon to close her eyes in ecstasy and sigh with rapture. . . . . .

But of all Danielli's collection of curiosities, the most genuine, the most pathetic and the most tragic, was an old, old woman. The very personification of misery— a silent reminder of the fickleness of fate, and of the relentlessness of time. A grotesque, weird and shrivelled old hag, in a silk dress that might have been fashionably new a half-century ago, she furtively limped her way from table to table offering roses for sale. She earned a fair sum, and more, for practically everyone patronized her, and, as at a church bazaar, there never was any change; nor did anyone ever complain at this. Perchance they looked upon her as the skeleton at the feast— and sought to purchase immunity from the ravages of the future. But the poor wretch spent her money as quickly as she made it, on drink— perhaps to drown her memories— perhaps to stimulate them, for she always grew most loquacious under the influence of alcohol, and many were the tales she had to tell of past splendours.

A curious head-gear covered her straggly, silver hair— a wreath of postal cards, depicting the old hag as she might have looked fifty or sixty years ago. She must have been amazingly beautiful. Beneath the pictures she had written, in a shaking, ill-formed hand:

> I used to rule as the Race-Track Queen—
> The friend of Emperors and Queens I've been—
> Emperors and Kings who have lost the race—
> Together with them I have lost my place!
> I beg you help me along.

"God bless you and keep you, and the young gentleman," she mumbled to Sonia, noting with her keen old eyes the sympathy in the girl's face. "And may you be married soon to all happiness, and to the coming of many happy little ones."

Sonia felt the hot flush rush to her cheeks. She looked quickly at Number 326. "Thank goodness, he hadn't heard!" He had taken all the flowers of the old harridan and was reaching for the money to pay for them. And yet, why should she flush? Was there anything she wanted more than the fulfillment of the old flower-seller's wish?

At the sight of the very generous payment for her wares, the old woman dropped a deep courtesy to Number 326, and bending again to Sonia, whispered: "Ye have trouble in your eyes, little lady. Put it from ye. It will not last." And mumbling, grinning, limping on her way, with a bit of repartee here and there, she passed bowing like a queen— she had no more flowers to sell— between the tables, her faded silk dress swishing softly along the floor as she flitted along, like a sere and withered autumn leaf blown by a fitful breeze.

"Why do you look so unhappy, beloved— that old woman?" whispered Number 326, caressing the girl's trembling arm. "We've found each other— what more can we want?"

"Yes! but how long can it last?" she whispered in return, her eyes following the old hag. "It *can't* last long enough!"

He could not answer except by the tender pressure on her cool bare arm.

"How long— if at all—" she repeated to herself.

Number 326 watched her fondle the roses he had given her, and saw her smile through her tears as she looked down on them.

"Come, dearest, let's dance. That is the only way I

can put my arms about you here. Oh! if I could only kiss you!" he added.

She arose quickly, and, laying the roses lovingly on the table, stood up before him. She was very beautiful in the exquisite evening gown, with the many lights glinting in her hair— her great eyes deep and unfathomable. She closed them as if in a trance when he put his arms around her and together they melted into the dance.

The orchestra was playing a languorous waltz, but wonderful as it was, she responded less to its swaying rhythm than to the music of the words he poured into her ears:

"Do you know what you remind me of, beloved?" he was saying earnestly. "Of a young linden just bursting into bloom for the first time— of a frozen rill that the touch of the early spring sun has awakened to life — of a little golden-haired kitten purring in the sun— yes that's it —there's something gloriously animal-like about you, Sonia. And you remind me, too, of a bird of passage that has grown too weary on its flight to go any farther. . . . I once saw such a bird. On a moonless, starless night, the sky thickly overcast, with the wind sighing mournfully through the lonely darkness, a flock of wild geese came flying rapidly across the lake.

They were trying to outdistance a threatening snow-storm. Their cries came loud and harsh across the water, as if they were encouraging each other with the sound of their voices. . . . Then, long after they had faded into the night, one lone bird appeared, flying wearily and nearly spent, so low over the surface of the lake that I thought I could see her hopeless eyes. I would have given a year of my life to have known how to imitate the call of those birds, in the chance that I might have lured her to me and have given her sanctuary. I have never been able to forget the note of terror and despair in that poor lost bird's cry as it struggled alone through the black night. . . . . ."

"Oh! my dearest," thought the girl. "If you only knew how much more I am like that little lost bird than your poetic linden tree or the purring kitten! And if you only knew how I long to end my own dark flight to heed the call of your dear voice and find sanctuary. Some day I can tell you all of my life. You will shudder, but you will listen, and your heart will ache no less for me than for the forsaken bird."

"Why, Sonia!— are you crying?" asked the man tenderly.

"I am so happy, dear, that's all— and I felt sorry for

your bird." She smiled at him through her tears, and trembled as she felt his lips touch her hair.

At the same moment she was conscious of another touch— someone had tapped her hand as it rested on the shoulder of her partner. Her eyes, filled with indignant resentment, met the leering glances of a *gigolo* who was keeping step with her. After several moments, he danced away behind the back of Number 326, but not until he had succeeded in slipping into her hand a tiny piece of paper.

No longer floating in a heavenly trance, she felt herself sinking— sinking into bottomless depths— she was being watched! Had she dared, she would have cried aloud for help, as the lost bird had done. . . . . .

Deftly, with a skill which made her despise herself, she unfolded the little roll of paper. To her ear came the whispered words of Number 326: "I love you, Sonia dearest,— I love you with all my heart and soul." To her eyes, the coded message blazed from the paper:

"You were due at Jellusic's over an hour ago!"

That was all— and it was more than enough.

"No escape. . . . no escape. . . ." blinked the myriad lights of the room as she danced on.

"No escape. . . . no escape. . . ." insisted the rhythm of the music

"No escape. . . . no escape. . . ." mocked the faces, the laughter, the eyes, the lips, the hands swarming about her, reiterating the horrid refrain:

"No escape. . . . no escape. . . . . !"

She was frantic. She closed her eyes, struggling for self-control, and rolled the vicious bit of paper into a small wad. She was shaking with bitter resentment. And all the while she was dancing, and he was holding her close and whispering to her— though his voice came as from a great distance— "Dearest, dearest, what a fool I have been. Only yesterday, I said that no woman would ever come into my life. I love you — I love you!"

She was almost strangling with self-disdain and contempt at herself for her fear, and yet her furious anger conquered. "I won't obey— I *won't* obey," she vowed, letting the crushed bit of paper fall under the feet of the passing dancers. "I won't obey! For the first time in my life, I am happy. I will not have it taken from me!"

She lifted her lovely head in her silent defiance— and stopped dead in the middle of a step, her eyes staring as though at a spectre.

There, at a small table sat Haghi; the stony-faced Petra behind his chair as ever!

"Dearest, dearest— what's the matter? You're white as a ghost." Number 326 was startled. He kept his arm about her to shield her from the dancing throng. "What's wrong, beloved?"

"Nothing— nothing, dear." The girl made a desperate effort to smile. "I'm all right— just a little faint."

"You look ready to drop. You've got to stop and sit down a minute or you *will* drop." He started to lead her to their table.

"I won't obey— I won't obey," she insisted to herself, and knew she was thinking a lie. "Dear God! we're going to pass right in front of Haghi— and he'll look at me!"

"No escape. . . . no escape. . . . . ."

But Haghi did not look at her. His cold eyes were fixed on the man with Sonia, and whose absorption in her was so complete that he was quite oblivious to his surroundings. Haghi stared, and Sonia felt that she could read the thoughts behind that impassive face: "So you are taking her away from me, are you? That may not be, young man. That woman belongs to me. She is the most valuable instrument I have. I do not tolerate others using what's mine. It displeases me to see that which belongs to me in the hands of others

. . . . I prefer to destroy it, and throw it away. . . . or
the person who tries to take it from me."

Sonia was now staring at Haghi, and praying, pleading that he would look at *her*. "Please, please!" she
was silently imploring. "Take your eyes away from
him— take your eyes away from him! . . . . I'll obey
— I'll go— I'll never rebel again— only don't look at
him like that."

But her silent prayers were unheard. Haghi seemed
to have eyes only for Number 326— sneering, threatening eyes— menacing, baleful eyes . . . . The girl's
hand reached for her throat. Her fingers closed on the
jewelled pendant which she wore suspended from a thin
gold chain. The fleeting shadow of a sudden resolve
crossed her face, and the slender chain snapped in her
hand. She let the costly gem slip unnoticed to the
floor, just as Haghi's glance shifted to hers.

He smiled quietly. "It would seem as if we really
understood each other now," his eyes seemed to say.

Sonia had barely strength to reach their table before
she collapsed. The head-waiter, he who had been the
Arch-Duke, he who was famous for his discretion,
gave the girl a hasty glance and hurriedly filled her glass
with champagne. Number 326 seized it from him, and
proffered it to the girl. She gulped it down, in the

hopes that the wine would bring her some strength. In a moment the colour returned to her cheeks, and she handed back the glass to the distressed man bending over her.

"It was only a passing faintness," she reassured him, reaching for her small evening-bag to get her handkerchief. "Oh! my dear," she exclaimed, "I had nearly forgotten! See, this is for you."

She held out to him a carved medallion of ivory; it was evidently an antique from the quaintness of the figure upon it— a figure representing some unknown feminine Saint.

"It has been the talisman of our family for generations," she said eagerly, "and must always be worn when travelling— it keeps away danger. It has always been given by our women to those they— they truly love. Sometimes others than—" she broke off sharply. "It came. . . . it came to me from my great-aunt, the one who gave me this. . . ." She raised her hand to her throat, and broke off in well-acted consternation. "My pendant!" she gasped, "I've lost my emerald pendant! I know I had it on while we were dancing. I felt it just a few minutes ago. . . . !" She jumped up in great distress. "It must have fallen off while . . . . oh! my dear, forgive me, if I'm so upset!"

"Don't— don't," he cried, "I'll find it— it's around somewhere." And rushed away— towards Haghi— towards Haghi!

Her burning eyes followed him for an instant only. She swayed against the table, and held to her chair for support. Then squaring her shoulders, she half-turned to the head-waiter. "My wrap, please," she said quickly.

He did not seem to understand her, although she had spoken distinctly enough. This former Arch-Duke, re-nowned for his discretion, stared at her almost rudely, not believing his ears. He flattered himself on his ability to judge people, and never had he served a guest who seemed less anxious to leave than this one. Sonia did not wait for him to adjust his psychology to meet the situation, but reaching quickly for her cloak, which was draped over the back of an adjoining chair, wrapped it hastily about her, and fled swiftly, without looking back.

The ex-Admiral of the late Imperial Navy, a trifle non-plussed, yet none the less graciously and condes-cendingly courteous, asked the lady who dashed so hurriedly out of Danielli's portal if he should call her motor. She shook her head, miserably, it seemed to him, and murmured distractedly: "A taxi, please, and hurry!"

The taxi drew up with a little street arab riding the running-board. He was one of the typical dirty little beggars who are always hanging around in the hopes of picking up a few pennies. He opened the door with a flourish, even before the taxi had come to a standstill. But Sonia had no eyes for him. Had the Angel Gabriel suddenly popped up from the pavement and flourished his trumpet in her face, she probably would not have seen him in that moment.

She stepped in quickly, giving the driver Jellusic's address. The starting jerk threw her into a corner of the seat, and there she remained huddled, unable to weep, and trembling in a violent nervous chill.

She did not dare to let her thoughts go back to the beloved man she had left alone at Danielli's— to think of what *his* thoughts would be when he returned to the table and found that she had again fled. "If unexplainable things happen!" Would he believe? No— no, she must not think of him! She must think of Jellusic— and her— *duty!* She spat the word from her. Suddenly, into the bewildered maze of her thoughts came the recollection that she was to meet Morrier. She leaned forward and hastily gave the driver the change of directions, and slumped again into her corner. She *was* in a hopeless corner. She found herself whimpering.

A slight jolt aroused her, and for a fleeting second she caught a glimpse of a sallow face framed in the taxi window— Morrier! His rat-like teeth flashed in the light of a street-lamp, as, with a flourish he tossed a heavy envelope into her lap, remarking with his inevitable smile twisted almost to a sneer: "You've certainly taken your time in getting here, haven't you?" and vanished into the night like an evil spirit. He was gone even before the letter, falling from her knees, had dropped to the floor. She stooped to pick it up, and opened it mechanically— like an automaton. Her thoughts were now on Morrier.

Morrier was not a man to be kept waiting without knowing why— unless under directions from his master. He had been told to await Sonia between 9:15 and 9:30, and she had not arrived until long after the appointed time. She knew that he would not rest until he could find the reason for the delay, and report it to Haghi. And then a strange relief came to her— Haghi already knew. There was nothing further to be feared from Morrier's certain search. She almost smiled at the thought of the hours this— this rat would spend in hopes of currying further favour with his master.

Her eyes ran over the contents of the envelope which her nerveless fingers had opened; it contained a thick package of bills and a code message addressed to her: a single, terrible sentence:

"You are forbidden to return to your own home."

Oh! God— could she bear any more? What did this last blow mean? Was Haghi about to strike at Him? Had he read in her soul the resolve that made the seduction of Number 326 impossible?

And where could she go now? Not openly to Him, for that would but bring upon them both a quick extermination. . . . Back to Haghi— to be seized and placed under constant surveillance— to be barred from any communication with Him. She *must* find Him again tonight. Somehow— some way. She would finish this loathsome business on hand— pay Jellusic his money for his plans and his treachery— mail the plans to Haghi, and with them her farewell. She would find Him— she would tell him all— she would appeal to his love, and to his faith in her— and they two would flee far beyond the reach of Haghi. If he had no money, her jewels would bring them enough.

Number 326 found the emerald pendant, which, almost miraculously, was unmarred despite the many dancing feet that had passed over and close to it. He hurried back to the table in his delight. It was deserted; his roses lay abandoned. Her wrap was gone.

The ex-Arch-Duke, standing close at hand, seemed to be struggling with that famous sense of discretion. He coughed, and cleared his aristocratic throat. Number 326 looked up at him, and years of reputation broke.

"The lady went on ahead, sir," he said, and it seemed that he could have bitten out his tongue the instant he had spoken. He glanced about in horror to see if anyone except Number 326 had heard his descent to "common gossip."

His words shocked Number 326 like ice-water thrown in his face. He tore a bank-note from his pocket, and without waiting for the change, rushed from the salon. That the ex-Arch-Duke was astounded may be gathered from the fact that he added the check again— and then again! He had been correct— he had made only his usual over-charge— his perquisite for deigning to serve the bourgeois— and yet this tip— colossal— the man must be mad!

And mad, or nearly so, he was. Number 326 did not stop even for his hat. He fought his way to the street through the in-coming guests. Yes, yes, the ex-Admiral doorman remembered the lady very well. She had gone off in a taxi— in a great hurry, and somewhat upset. . . . No he had not heard the address.

Franz drove up. His master asked him the same questions. The chauffeur was bitter in his self-criticism. He had scarcely believed his eyes when he had seen the lady rush out all alone, but before he could gather his senses she had driven off in a taxi— in that direction— but the Lord only knows where to.

Chagrined though he was at his failure to aid his beloved master, Franz found a certain consolation in the fact that now, at least, one of his set remarks fitted perfectly. He did not utter it aloud, even his satisfaction was not so rash as that, but as he opened the door of the car he muttered to himself: "I told you so— I *told* you so!"

As Number 326 turned to enter the car he stopped. A hand clutched his arm. Looking down, he saw an unbelievably grimy paw, the owner of which, standing on a pair of equally filthy bare legs, was grinning from ear to ear.

"Say, Mister," he offered, "I kin tell you where the lady went to."

Number 326 grabbed him fiercely by both arms.

"Quick, quick— where did she go?"

The boy, with a movement that would have awakened the envy of an eel, slipped from his grasp, and danced away to a safe distance. "Nothin' doin' on the strong-arm stuff, Mister. What'll ye give to find out— and pay in advance. I ain't goin' to get stuck a second time. The lady stung me. I opened her door and she didn't give me nothin'. You can pay first."

Number 326 reached for his money, and handed the gamin a bank-note that made the youngster's eyes nearly start from their sockets.

"Where did she go?" repeated Number 326.

"She told the chauffeur to go to— Mister I've got good ears and I've got some sense I have, and what's more I know the place— it's a rummy hole, Mister— I knows, I live in that alley myself— Ye'd better take a club along if you're goin'."

"Yes— damn you, but where is it?"

"Don't you hold me so if you want to know— bend down Mister— and don't let them others hear."

But Number 326 was already in the car, and Franz, having heard the address, speeded up as soon as the door closed.

The speculations of the small gamin on why a beautiful lady should rush off in a taxi to the slums in which he lived, and why a hatless young man should rush after her in a marvellous car, were rudely inter- rupted by the unsuccessful attempt of the ex-Admiral to snatch the bank-note from him. "Try somethin' easier, old gold lace an' whiskers," he jeered, as he easily avoided the naval manœuvres, "I ain't no gov- ernment that you can pick money from me that way."

CHAPTER VII

A DESCENT INTO HELL

No. 17 Dawn St., was a fifth, or n'th, class hotel, situated in a blind alley into which no automobile could turn. It was a dirty narrow building with a glass door up to which led two filthy broken-down steps. A feeble light glimmered over the entrance, faintly showing a sign which set forth the information that rooms could be rented at all hours, and for any length of time.

The suite-de-luxe of this establishment was furnished in brilliant red plush, further enhanced by many soiled crocheted tidies. It boasted a screen made entirely of picture postals, for the most part salacious, and flaunted crude chromos of a less than doubtful nature on its tattered and dirty walls. Its present, and to do him justice temporary, occupant was Colonel Mirko Jellusic.

Col. Jellusic was an exceptionally brilliant and clever man and officer. As a man, he had found no great difficulties in the way of a complete enjoyment of life. Tall, well set-up, even handsome, except for a suggestion of effeminacy— although his marvellously long and rigidly waxed moustache was the envy of his fellow-officers— he met with no difficulty with Women or women. He was most generous and extravagant, and this failing he had found incompatible with a Colonel's pay. The joys of life, he would not give up— therefore it behooved him to add to his income. As Colonel on the Headquarters Staff, he had acquired a reputation, which was deserved, and achieved a trust which was not; and through his position he soon found an easy way of increasing the income necessary to "maintain his position."

Probably the first step across that line which divides honour and dishonour had been hard to make— but that had been years ago. Now, his negotiations with several representatives of other nations had settled into a regular and lucrative "profession." And, to give the lie to the old adage, this big handsome man, at whom women smiled so readily— this traitor and scoundrel— slept as calmly at night as a healthy child.

He greeted Sonia with courteous deference, and a concealed smile of satisfaction. It pleased him to have a beautiful woman seen entering his apartment at this hour— and he made no effort to conceal his admiration for the girl herself. To keep the appointment, he had come direct from the gaming table where he, as usual, had lost more than he could afford. To be sure, there had been compensations for these losses— women, caresses and wine— wonderful champagne they had there! The women he had left, the caresses were forgotten, but the champagne was with him yet, and he was in high humour and bubbling spirits. So much so, that he evinced a disconcerting disinclination to talk business. More wine, and song— and here was woman!

He reached out for Sonia's bare arms, which he tried to fondle with his hot, moist hands. Under the pretext that she was greatly pressed for time, Sonia moved out of his range, and, quickly unwrapping the bundle of bank-notes, laid them before him. He did not notice her shudder of repugnance as her hand approached his, and she failed to appreciate the tremendous tribute to her beauty that Mirko Jellusic paid in giving but a passing glance to the small fortune she had spread on the table between them, and raising his admiring eyes to hers.

"Colonel Jellusic, I must report back to headquarters within fifteen minutes," she lied, catching her

breath in her disgust. "Your train leaves in less than
four hours, and you are fully aware of the conditions
of this transaction; you must cross the frontier before
day-break! Shall we close the matter, Colonel? Here
is the twenty thousand pounds!"

Jellusic stood looking down at her rather mournfully,
twisting the waxed ends of the moustache of which
he was so proud. He saw the money in her hands,
for Sonia had been careful to keep it within her reach,
and had now picked it up again, and he saw the woman.
Less than a month ago, he might have made the mistake of trying to seize both the money and the woman,
but since that time he had learned a humiliating lesson— a similar attempt had ended most ignominiously
for him as he looked at the wrong end of a revolver.
He nurtured no warm desire to repeat that experience,
and, he noticed that Sonia, while holding the notes in
one hand, kept the other hand in the pocket of her
wrap.

"Have it your way, Sonia," he assented, shrugging
his shoulders. "Let's make the exchange, and get
business done with. Will there ever be a man who'll
appeal to that cold beauty of yours, Sonia?"

She was silent.

From a brief-case lying on a near-by chair, Jellusic

He threw a careless glance at the money, then resumed his admiring attention.

drew a bundle of papers, and returned to the table. Clutching these firmly in his hand, he held them out to the woman opposite. She, in turn, reached forward the notes for twenty thousand pounds. Each seized simultaneously the offering of the other, and there was an equally simultaneous release. "Honesty among thieves? . . . ." thought Sonia cynically.

She slipped the papers into a secret pocket in her coat-sleeve, while Jellusic ran rapidly through the notes. It was merely a matter of form; intelligent merchants do not short-change their customers— if they are expecting to deal with them in the future.

"And now, good-bye, Colonel Jellusic," said Sonia, folding her cloak close to her throat.

He looked at her, and sighed. "And for how long, Sonia?"

She gazed at him thoughtfully. "That is something, Colonel, that I cannot answer. I suppose it all depends on whether there are any more secrets left in your country that are worth buying and that you can offer for sale. . . . If there are, I am quite sure it won't be long before we meet again."

The man's face set, his eyes narrowed, and his smile stiffened.

"I shall escort you to the door," he said briefly.

SPIES

Holding her cloak tightly about her, to avoid any possible contact with the filthy walls, the girl followed him down the narrow dark stairs. The mouldy smell, the dirty creaking steps, the dim light filtering through the dust and fly-specks on the electric bulb sickened her. "Thank God! this was the last time!"

Jellusic unlatched the glass-panelled door, but suddenly barred her way. With his best ingratiating smile, and a preparatory twist of his beautiful moustache: "And, now, dear lady, since we are about to part for a long time, shall we not indulge ourselves in a tender embrace of farewell?"

As he spoke, he stepped quickly forward and seized her in his arms. She fought with all the strength of her splendid youth, aided by the anger of a woman deeply in love who is defiled by the touch of a man other than her own. She steeled herself against his attack— she even succeeded in hurling him against the wall, but could not break his hold. Back and forth they swayed, his hot mouth seeking hers, his lips pressing her shoulders and throat again and again. She fought like a trapped lioness, until, freeing one arm, she struck him full on the ear with her clenched fist. With a gasp of pain, he released her. Tearing open the door, she dashed down the steps into the street.

A DESCENT INTO HELL

Standing aghast, not ten paces away, was Number 326— bare-headed, with ashen face— staring—staring in petrified horror at the woman who had dashed from that sordid building, her hair disordered, her flaming face besmudged, her gown and wrap slipping from her shoulders— and behind her, framed in the open doorway, a man in a dressing-gown, which plainly revealed his unbuttoned, and rumpled shirt! And, this man was smiling— that it was a rather rueful smile was not evident— and carefully twisting into position the displaced points of a waxed moustache.

With a great cry of relief, Sonia ran toward the man she loved— the man who would protect her— save her, and shrank back in terror before the distorted face that even his own mother would not have recognized. She did not hear the bitter words of his mad denunciation— the tone of his voice was enough! With a despairing moan, she broke into a run past him; and he drew back from her as from a venomous snake. On and on, she ran— faster and faster— she knew not where. Her only thought was to get away as far as she could. At the corner, she spied a vacant taxi into which she flung herself. . . . the door slammed. . . . the car exploded into action. . . . . .

Number 326 did not pursue the fleeing car— he was

not thinking then of following this woman who had changed his life and then had wrecked it— all within twenty-four hours. The whirl of his dizzied brain centered not on the woman, but on that man in the doorway!

Mirko Jellusic had watched, with a certain amount of relish, the scene which had been enacted before him privately, as if he were Royalty itself. He loved excitement of any sort, whether he took an active or a passive part in it. He was not a coward— merely a traitor to his country in order that he might be a better servant to his own needs. He flattered himself that he could, as a rule, anticipate the moves of his adversaries— he had done so for several years— but the vehemence and speed with which Number 326 hurled himself into the entrance of the doorway upset his calculations entirely. Number 326 was too quick for him. He had cleared the steps and jammed his foot in the door before Jellusic had time to close it in his face.

"What was that woman doing here— in this— this house?" he demanded fiercely.

Mirko Jellusic looked down pityingly at the distracted young man. The fellow was clearly labouring under a delusion. Why should he be enlightened? His evident deduction suited Jellusic very well— it covered up the real reason for Sonia's visit; and besides, the inference was flattering— a proper tribute to his fascination for beautiful women. He shrugged his shoulders, and replied blandly: "My dear Sir, whom I have not the pleasure of knowing, I cannot see that it is in any way a business of yours; and, also, a gentleman does not discuss with strangers the— er— ladies who visit his rooms." He smiled smugly, caressing the wonderful moustache.

Number 326 tottered back. His arms fell limp to his sides. . . . He understood. . . . No! . . . . it couldn't be. . . . he didn't understand. . . . Fool! . . . . he did. . . . of course he did! The street began to heave before his eyes, twisting like a great snake— the tumble-down houses swayed— their black shadows leered at him— horrible, insinuating leers. . . . The doorway receded, and the smirking foreigner framed in it grew thinner and thinner until he was but a thread. A dizzying roar filled his ears. The creak of the closing door aroused him, but the bolt had been shot with a rasp, and the dirty, fly-specked light snapped out.

Number 326 attacked the door frantically, for a moment tempted to smash in the grimy panels, the glass through which he had seen, a few minutes before, two human bodies silhouetted as they swayed back and forth in close embrace. Sonia's face flashed before him. He saw her as she had left that man— she, the woman whom a few short hours ago he had held so tenderly in his own arms. . . . saw her fleeing down the crooked steps of the sordid building— "a rummy district, Mister!"— her face distorted, her clothes torn from her shoulders, her hair awry and flying in the wind as she had rushed past him down that foul street— her face— the face he had thought so candid and innocent— which had inspired in him such admiration and faith, and for the first time in his life awakened in his soul love and adoration— her face stamped with horror!

Great God! Was he going mad?

And then rage swept over him. The woman had made a fool of him! She was probably laughing to herself at his gullibility— at the ease with which he had fallen for her snares. Nearly insane with fury, he tore open the door of his car, snapping at Franz the address of her house.

The devoted servant opened the throttle wide. He did not need to be told that his beloved master was in extreme haste. "He has never before been like this," he thought, taking a corner on two wheels. "May that woman be damned!— I told you so, I told you so."

A DESCENT INTO HELL

Her house! A short twelve hours ago the shrine which he had entered with awe, reverence and devotion— the house that sheltered the woman he had loved, idealized and worshipped . . . . and now? It was as he leaped from the car that a consoling thought flashed into his mind: Had she been forced to tear herself from his tenderness and love . . . . had she been driven to that vile den from which he had seen her emerge like a maniac . . . . was she facing dangers of which he knew nothing . . . . was this all, perhaps, the first blow of the unknown fiend he had been set to find and fight? Had this ruthless devil struck at him through the woman he loved? And then, with a sweeping re-surge, the question: "was the woman hand-in-glove with this adversary?" By heaven he would get at the truth, and from the woman herself!

"Thank the Lord!" exclaimed Franz as he wiped the cold sweat from his face— and, then, he saw the look on his master's face.

Number 326 was standing on the sidewalk, staring in consternation at the little house.

It was deserted!

Under a threatening sky, that glowed a dull red from the reflection of the city lights, the small building stood in utter darkness,— in evident abandonment. A sinister sense of danger seemed to radiate from it, repelling him. The naked windows, stripped of their curtains, glared at him, in the light of the street-lamp, with a diabolical derision.

Number 326 aroused himself with an effort and went up to the door. He rang the bell. There was no answer except the echo from an obviously empty house. He rang again, nearly driving the button into the wall. No answer! Not a sign of life in the house — no voice, no footstep, no light, no creak of a door. Nothing but dead, black silence!

Setting his teeth, and with an oath, he flung himself against the door. He fell through, nearly to the floor beyond— the door was unlatched, and yielded unresistingly. Had it been left open purposely? Number 326 hesitated a moment, to take his pistol in one hand and his spotlight in the other. Then, he stepped forward. He would have welcomed resistance.

The house was nothing but an empty shell— stripped, cleaned bare. He remembered every detail of the tiny entrance-hall, as he had seen it that afternoon, when the surly maid had admitted him. His mind had been carefully trained to register and to record everything which he saw or heard— he had made a private game of it; like Lurgan Sahib's game in Kipling's *Kim*— and recollected where each chair had stood, where each picture had hung— the shaded lights, the crystal mirror on the wall opposite the door . . . . and, now, nothing!

The spirit of the little house was dead; and the desiccated corpse of it— a cold, deserted, abandoned thing— alone remained in the blackness and silence.

The light that filtered in through the iron grill from the street-lamp outside, threw grotesque shadows on the bare walls. Nothing but the faintly illusive suggestion of the fragrance of roses left a trace to show that, but a few hours ago, this had been the charmingly furnished dwelling of a fastidious gentlewoman.

Through the rooms, Number 326 rushed in a futile endeavour to find some sign— some clue. His spotlight raced around each empty chamber, only to reveal the hopelessness of his search. Blankness, bareness — except for the hanging light-wires, from which even the fixtures had been torn.

Number 326 never knew how long he was in that deserted house, nor how he at length came to drag himself from it. He could remember nothing clearly now. "Oh! yes!— Sonia . . . . she was . . . . what had she been doing there . . . . that man . . . . he

must . . . . what was it he had to do . . . . Sonia
. . . . empty . . . . what a dream. . . . . ."

("When he breaks, he will break badly!")

He found a strangely familiar car in front of him,
with a man at the wheel whom he had seen before,
and whom for some unknown reason he addressed as
"Franz"— This man was speaking to him— pleading with him to come home. Why should he go home
with this strange Franz man? He looked dully at
him— he couldn't see very well. He turned on his
spotlight— shot it fully into the face of this Franz.
Yes, he had seen him somewhere before— but what
was the use of trying to remember. He gave it up,
and with a shrug shambled off down the street.

He did not notice the car following him at a distance. The sky was overcast— rain was in the air.
"That'll be cool," he thought, clapping his hand to his
hot, hatless head. The wind blew in short gusts, and
tossed his hair into dishevelled confusion. He jammed
his hands into his pockets, and walked on. That was
what he wanted to do— walk. But he wasn't walking.
The whole town was rushing by him while he stood
still, except for moving his feet— if the houses only
wouldn't whirl by so fast. Was that a bell— a great
gong ringing, sounding, deafening him? Hark to

the beat: Sonia .... Sonia .... Sonia! Who
was Sonia? Oh! yes, she was that woman!

Who had struck him .... his head ached ....
someone had hit him .... someone was counting
him out: four, five, six, seven— No, that wasn't it, it
was he himself counting his own footsteps. What
time was it? Where was he? He had been walking
for thousands of hours— endless hours. Why didn't
they clean the streets in this city— and wash the walls
of the houses? Every time he brushed against a wall
he got all dirty. What a filthy place— he'd better go
somewhere.

Suddenly he was conscious of music blaring from a
nearby doorway. The sound of voices reached him,
and he heard fists beating time to the rhythm of a vul-
gar song that was being ground out by a rasping
phonograph. He could distinguish the drunken cater-
wauling of a woman, high above the general din, and
heard the roars of raucous laughter provoked, probably, by some foul story. He caught his breath, and
listened; a beastly leer distorted his face.

This was what he needed— his head was partially
clearing— this was what he needed— now he remembered— he would go where he had given his heart— to
filth, to scum— to the sewer. There's where he'd feel at

home now! He kicked open the baize door, and stumbled into the dive.

Swaying in the narrow doorway, he offered an incongruous picture in that foul place; for, despite his dishevelled condition, the dinner coat, dirtied as it was, the expanse of nearly white shirt-front seemed in contrast to the surroundings to be the extreme of gentility.

The room into which he had stepped was heavy with stale tobacco-smoke and the fumes of bad beer and worse wine. Women, coarsely painted to conceal even coarser faces, women whose profession was only too evident, lolled at the tables trying to get their "escorts" to buy another drink— on which they received a percentage— or danced lewdly to the horrid cacophony of the phonograph. No one payed the slightest attention to Number 326.

A huge negro sat behind the cashier's grill. On the counter beside him lay a pistol, and a heavy club. In the wall of his cage to his left was a door that could be opened only from the inside, but which swung wide at the touch of a foot-pedal, thus enabling this black giant to leap forth with his pistol in one hand, and his club in the other.

As Number 326 elbowed his way through the

drunken dancers to the table where he collapsed, the bulky figure of the ethiopian proprietor stepped to his side. The "what'llyeh've" question was lost in the crash of glass from the other side of the room, as two girls, each very young, and both very faded, stabbed at each other with the weapons they had made of the glasses from which they had been drinking the negro's poison. It was but an instant! The black mountain bending over Number 326 hurled itself across the room — the girls were seized, one in each huge hand, and tossed through the swinging doors to the pavement outside. "Clean up that glass," ordered the negro to a cringing sweeper, and, ignoring entirely the wild cheers of his drunken assembly, returned to Number 326.

"What'llyehave?"

Number 326 raised his befuddled head and stared in amazement at the black face hanging over his. "Nothing— nothing," he mumbled, and immediately, "no— yes, I mean— a quart of Scotch, and be quick about it." That was it— he would get drunk— hopelessly— and rest— and forget! What was it that he wanted to forget? He was so tired. . . . If the cotton would only keep away— the balls of cotton that whirled round in crazy circles inside his head— if they would only make a noise when they bumped against each

other— but they were too soft— they were like
thoughts— they couldn't make a noise. That was it
he couldn't have thoughts— they were crazy things—
they drove men mad— insane— Sonia . . . . Sonia.
. . . Always insane . . . . it was inevitable . . . .
how his eyes burned . . . . "a rummy district, Mister!" Damn that nigger . . . . here was the whiskey.

. . . . .

Glass after glass of the poison the negro sold for
whiskey poured down the throat of Number 326.
"That nigger should be hanged for this!" . . . . and
then another glass, and still another. Even a habitué
cannot consume a quart of bad liquor without becoming fuddled, and yet the vicious stimulant seemed to
clear the mind of Number 326. His rapid gulping
slowed to a mechanical sipping, and ceased, with a
half-full glass before him.

With the automatic movement of the drinker or
the tippler, his hand reached out again for the glass.
He felt another hand upon his. He raised his sodden
eyes, and found himself looking into a yellow face.
"What a nightmare! What a nightmare— ," and he
ran his hands desperately through his hair, to clear
his mind— "women that lie— sneering men— negroes

— Chinamen or Japs— oh! God!" His head slumped into his hands.

From a great distance there came a voice, and, with the voice, a further clearing of the fog in his brain. Again, automatically, his hand reached for the bottle.

"Don't!" said a voice— and it was that of one used to authority— "Don't! You have much to do, and this," he hurled the bottle on the floor, "will not help you!"

At the crash of the glass, the giant negro leaped from behind his embrasure to meet the imperturbable look of the Oriental, and rebound from it. "I ask your pardon, sir," he pleaded, servilely. A dignified bow of the head was his acknowledgment.

Slowly and deliberately, as though it were quite the natural thing for him to be doing, and without releasing his hold upon the hand of Number 326, this stranger from the other side of the world seated himself. "Don't drink any more of that!" He spoke in a soothing voice, enunciating the words with the distinctness of a foreigner.

Number 326 frowned at him. He squinted his eyes in an attempt to focus them. Where had he seen this man before— this was not the first time that he had looked into that determined, gentle face, with its jet-black eyes, inscrutable with the mystery of the East.

"Yes," he said quietly, in answer to the puzzled look of Number 326, "you have seen me before—last night, in the Olympic. We— opened our doors at the same time."

The last sentence sobered Number 326— for a moment his brain functioned again— the man across the hall— the Oriental of the strange warning! "Yes! I remember," he snapped. "You warned me of something— Who are you?"

"I am Dr. Matsumoto," replied the stranger, "perhaps even the Secret Service may have heard of me. Don't be startled, my dear boy. I know well who you are, and if you had been your famous self for the past twenty-four hours you would know all about me. I ask that you understand this: we are fighting the same adversary, although for different reasons— I can help you, and you can help me. I know no more who he is than you do, but I *do* know one of his trusted assistants. I followed you here from her deserted house!"

Number 326 leaped to his feet in seething anger— the more violent, perhaps, because of this corroboration of his most bitter suspicions.

A DESCENT INTO HELL

"Need I tell you that anger is always futile," came the quiet voice, "and anger at the truth is worse than foolish. My boy, you and I have experienced great disappointments to-night— and you more than that— a horrible disillusionment. I beg of you not to let it deter you from your pledged duty— not to let the bitterness in your heart turn you from your work. Duty is not always pleasant— it is mine to tell you, now, that you are not the first to have been duped by this fascinating woman— this super-spy— the most valuable tool of the devil we both must fight.

"That empty house to-night was a tragedy to you, but it was merely a personal one— to me, it was international. Had she been there, she would now have been under arrest, and one cannot tell to what that might have led. A marvellous— a most astounding organization indeed— that protects her."

Number 326, transfixed, stared at the kindly, troubled face opposite. He pushed aside the nearly empty whiskey glass as he leaned across the table. The momentary clarity of mind did not last, he had had too much of the horrible poison that the negro sold as Scotch. He could only mumble stupidly: "A spy. . . . A spy. . . . !" and he repeated the word dully, over and over again.

"Yes," said the doctor, gently, "a spy. Sonia Nikolovena Baranikowa is a remarkable spy. . . . It is almost a pleasure to be duped by her— a pleasure which many have experienced."

Number 326 suddenly threw back his head, and began to laugh; softly, at first, as if to himself, but his bitter mirth rose quickly to a horrible choking laughter that fairly burst from his aching throat. He shook with a vehemence that racked him. The lips which she had kissed so tenderly were drawn back and twisted— the hands she had so lovingly caressed— the head she had so gently stroked, trembled and quivered.

"A Spy!" he strangled, the hysterical tears streaming down his face. "She— A SPY!"

The events of the past twenty-four hours flashed before him like the crazy projections of a film that has slipped off the reel, speeding across the screen in mad distortion. Picture after picture raced dizzily by: of her, rushing into his rooms . . . . her fainting . . . . her sudden flight . . . . the brief note she had left behind . . . . the letter with which she had lured him to her home . . . . her caresses . . . . their dance . . . . the lost jewel . . . . the rotter at that doorway from which she had fled . . . . the deserted house . . . . all a plan— a plot, of which he had been the

easy dupe, of a wonderful spy— a super-spy . . . .
Sonia. . . . Sonia. . . . . .

His laughter broke suddenly with a gasp— he reeled for an instant, and, completely spent, collapsed, his head dropping upon his arms outspread across the table-top.

The doctor had watched with a great sympathy in the deep eyes hidden behind the enormous spectacles— and had waited with true Oriental patience for the subsiding of the emotional explosion. They two were now alone in the saloon, for the bank-note with which Dr. Matsumoto had paid for his orangeade and three words spoken in an undertone to the huge negro had sufficed to close up the place. Even the phonograph had been silenced. The lingering clouds of tobacco smoke were drifting reluctantly toward the door. The fumes of the spilled whiskey rose from the foul floor.

Dr. Matsumoto placed his cool dry hands over the feverish ones of the European, who winced as though touched on an open wound.

"There is not a woman in the world," he began quietly, "who is worth the ruin of a man's life—especially when his life does not belong to him, but to his duty. The man who has a mission to fulfill does not own his own life."

Number 326 slowly raised his head and listened—
it was like the chant of the Litany. On and on went
the subdued voice, the voice of a man of culture and
breeding, uttering the knowledge and philosophy of one
of much experience and deep thought— of one who
never condemns because of his great understanding.
The mellow voice calmed and soothed him. "And,
now," concluded the doctor, "we shall go out and find
the good Franz who is waiting for you, and he will
take you to your bed, where you will sleep, my boy,
sleep and forget. In the morning, after you have reported to my good friend Jason, perhaps you will come
and talk to me— here is my address— for I have
done all the talking to-night; I may help you in your
duty and your work— for, behind this beautiful woman
is the man whom I must fight and that you must find."

Franz was horror-stricken at the appearance of his
beloved master, but at a sign from the Doctor, merely
opened the door of the car. "Franz, will see you to
bed," he spoke more to the chauffeur than to Number
326, "safely in bed, and will stay by you until you
are sound asleep— with no dreams. Good-night."
He stepped back, releasing the feverish grip of Number 326, and, with a significant glance at Franz, motioned him to go.

CHAPTER VIII

KITTY

THE first drops of the threatening thunderstorm began to fall as the Japanese turned to cross the street. By the time he had reached the other side, the driving downpour was on. Dr. Matsumoto turned up the collar of his raincoat, pulled his hat down over his eyes and struggled against the gale that swept along the storm. He was happy— rain always made him pathetically happy. It reminded him of the incessant slanting showers that poured from the clouds mantling the sacred Fujiyama. Rain took him back to his land— his people, hopping over the puddles on high-heeled flopping clogs, their legs showing bare under their straw coats. He could hear the inimitable and unforgettable sighing of the wind in the fir trees and the temple bells, and he seemed to inhale the fragrance of the plum and cherry-trees opening their blossoms.

143

He walked on with a steady stride. Taxis slowed
as they passed him to give this belated wanderer a
chance to hail them— but he did not see the cars. Before his homesick eyes sped a procession of rickshaws
drawn by their two-legged beasts of burden, passing
with rapid ease between the thousands who crowded
the narrow streets, because every one politely, and with
gentle apologetic gestures, made room. Rice fields
beckoned to him. Men and women, knee-deep in
water, bent over the ripening grain. He heard the cry
of the bird of ill-omen, and saw a little girl try to
chase it from her garden by the clapping of her hands.

He could not get the cry of the bird nor the voice
of the child from his ears, as with half-closed eyes he
fought his way through the rain. Suddenly he stopped
short. He could still hear the voice of a child— but
this was weeping. He turned in the direction whence
it came.

Huddled in a doorway that offered her little protection from the storm, he found a girl. For a moment,
he thought she was indeed a child, but quickly saw
that this was budding maidenhood instead. She was
dripping wet and shivering with cold— in complete
physical misery. She was weeping hopelessly, her
hands covering her face, but she jumped up in wild

144

alarm as Dr. Matsumoto leaned over her, and touched her shoulder. At the sight of the strange face with its big spectacles bending over her, she shrieked as though she had seen a devil, and crept into the farthest corner of the doorway. A little box of water-soaked matches fell from her sodden lap. She seemed too frightened to utter another sound, and clapped her hands to her face in abject fear. The man, in his kindly sympathetic voice, offered to help her, but the girl did not seem to hear. Her small body trembled violently under its covering of rags that she had long since out-grown. Her shoes were many sizes too large for her, almost falling from her small naked feet. Her eyes blinked with the movements of those of a terrified bird— a small wild bird that has been caught.

Gradually she seemed to understand. She raised her head slightly, and listened to this soothing voice that was uttering such words of kindness and sympathy. She turned slowly toward him— this gentle man— as a flower turns toward the sun. Her expression of terror gradually subsided, and her fears faded.

"What is your name, my child?" asked the man.

"Kitty."

"And where do you live?"

Her terror leapt again to her face. She would not

tell him. . . . She would never go back . . . . she would rather die!

Quietly, he drew her story from her: her father, a bestial drunkard, a beating brute— her mother even worse, with but one interest in life— gin. Her "home" was a mouldy cellar. She slept on the steps— the only place she could get away from her mother, and in consequence usually suffered from her father's drunken rage when he stumbled over her. She would never go back!

"But, you cannot stay here, my child," said the man. "Would you like to come home with me?"

She looked up at him, her eyes filled with tears, as if to see what new horrors this suggestion might bring.

Dr. Matsumoto did not ask any more questions. He opened his coat, stooped down, picked up the dripping girl and wrapped her in its folds. Trembling, her big eyes fastened themselves on the man's face, but she submitted without resistance. With a pathetic movement, she reached for the ruined matches, which were almost floating in the rain.

"Leave them, my child," smiled Dr. Matsumoto, "I'll pay you for them."

It was evident that she could not understand this strange man, but she obeyed. She seemed to have made up her suspicious little mind to trust him. He bent and buttoned the rain coat about her. Her small feet, lost in the great torn shoes, splashed through the puddles as she endeavoured to keep step with him. The Doctor, having turned up his coat collar, was walking perhaps a trifle fast; his house was but a few doors away, and the rain was teeming. Suddenly, a slim hand slipped into his made him forget the rain and the discomfort of the wetting.

"Here we are, my child," he smiled reassuringly, "and we'll have you dry and warm and fed in just a moment or two."

It was a large house, whose threshold few people had passed; and still fewer had seen it in its entirety. There was nothing in its reception-rooms to indicate that this was the abode of an Oriental. Quite the contrary, these rooms were most conventionally furnished, and lacked all personality, as if the owner took little interest in them. From these rooms, one got the instinctive impression that the man who lived in this house regarded it merely as a very temporary dwelling-place— not as a home.

No servants were in evidence when Dr. Matsumoto, and the small waif entered. The man took entire charge of the girl himself. He first prepared a hot bath for her, as she seemed to need that above all things. She sat watching him in silent fascination, glued to the edge of her chair, like a tiny wet mud-swallow.

"Now, wash yourself thoroughly, little one," he encouraged, with his gentle voice. "Scrub yourself hard, from head to foot."

His house contained no feminine apparel, so he replaced the dripping rags the girl had worn with some of his own native garments— exquisitely fine cashmere robes of softest weave, in black and white. His kindly face wreathed itself in smiles, when, after a lengthy bath, the girl slipped into the living-room wearing these clothes— a hesitant, eerie little figure that might have stepped out of a Japanese fairy-tale. The ample folds, that fell over her feet in such a droll manner, she held as best she could, apparently endeavouring to keep them from dragging on the floor.

Dr. Matsumoto had already made up for her a bed on the divan, and had placed beside it a low table on which was tea and pastry. Next to it glowed an electric heater.

"Come over here, little woman, and warm yourself," he cried, almost gayly. "Warm yourself and eat."

She obeyed in silence, as her furtive glances ran

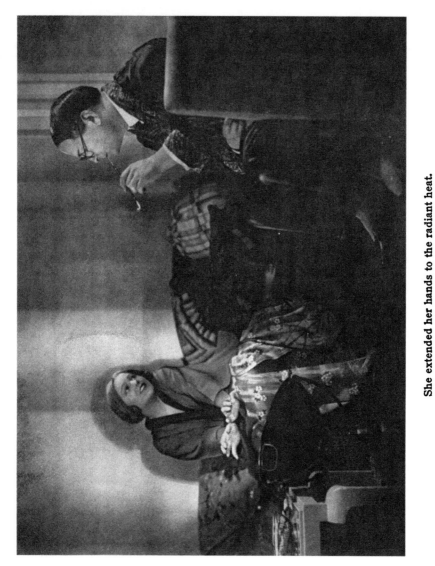

She extended her hands to the radiant heat.

about the room, to rest finally in apparent complete confidence in this strange creature— a man who was kind! She blinked at the stove, she extended her small hands toward the warmth, and seduced by the comfort the tiny feet crept also toward the glow. "Like a stray kitten," thought the man.

He sat back in his arm-chair and watched her. Her short hair, which had been plastered to her head by the rain, had also been washed, and was now drying rapidly. It was as fine as silk, and a wonderful ashen blonde. His hand reached out to touch it, as one would feel a silken embroidery, but the girl raised her head at the moment, and something in the happy innocence of her smile made him draw back.

"Why aren't you eating?" he asked, clearing his throat. "You are letting your tea grow cold."

Obediently, she reached for the handleless cup, and, with a natural grace, lifted it to her lips. She ate the food too, daintily, and rapidly, like a bird. Again and again, she stretched out her hands to the golden glow of the heater. Her half-hidden face was suffused with a soft rose flush by its friendly warmth, and her lips, still moist from the tea, parted in a contented smile, showing her even white teeth.

Suddenly, as though she had heard a voice, she

151

raised her eyes, and met the gaze of the man, who was looking at her with an expression of troubled wonder. She knelt down, and pressed her head shyly, and yet with an appealing trust, against his hand, and rubbed her cheek against it. She apparently was, in her innocence, ignorant of the fact that her loose garment had slipped from her shoulders, and that her slender form, glowing rosy from its recent bath and the warmth of the heater, was exposed in all its exquisite loveliness.

The man's hand rested without moving under her chin, but when she bent her lips to it he quickly twitched it away. He replaced it in a moment on her silken head, and almost immediately rose from his chair. The girl looked at him, startled and mystified. She carelessly pulled about her the loose folds of the garments, and her little face fell.

"Have I made you angry?" she cried, in distress. "Why did you jump away from me like that?"

Dr. Matsumoto did not answer. He pocketed his pipe, and passed his hand very slowly over his forehead. The room grew very still. The Japanese regarded the girl in strained silence— a silence that seemed unending.

"Are you going to send me away," asked Kitty, at

last. Her voice was weak with weariness, and yet seemed to bespeak her willingness to abide by the wishes of her benefactor.

"No," replied the man, slowly. "You may stay with me here as long as you wish, little Kitty. And, now, it is time for you to be asleep."

Obediently she slipped down on the divan, and curled herself among the cushions. He stooped to cover her up. One slim arm slid from the wide sleeve and about his neck, the motion again displacing the kimono and revealing the exquisite body it should have concealed. "Why have you been so good to me?" she cried, and lifted her face to him in a quick kiss.

He turned away his eyes, and snapped off the light. The glow of the heater alone shone through the room.

"Good-night,— good-night, my child," he said huskily. He hesitated a second or more at the door, his hand holding the knob; then, staring ahead with a forced, weary smile, he shook his head, and walked slowly to his own room.

About five minutes after Dr. Matsumoto and little Kitty had entered the house of the Japanese, Haghi, sitting at his desk in the great stone room, lifted the telephone.

"Morrier, Chief," the voice over the wire spoke, "Kitty's made it— she's inside."

"Report to-morrow," ordered Haghi, and motioned Petra to wheel him from the room.

CHAPTER IX

FROM A PRISON CELL

MY most dearly Beloved: I am writing this letter
while held a prisoner. I am writing it in my little
pocket note-book, as that is the only thing I have, and
I must write with such tiny letters that you will have
to use a magnifying glass to read it. I write without
knowing whether this will ever reach you, for I am
surrounded by the most astounding system of guards
— no one could elude them. And I write without having much hope that you still love me enough even to
read this letter should it actually reach you. Nevertheless, I must write, I must tell you. What else is
there for me to do if I am not to go raving mad.

I found you— and I lost you, my Beloved.

You trusted me and you think that I betrayed you.
Dear God in Heaven! where shall I find the words
that will restore your faith in me? I understand now
why, in days gone past, women whose fidelity was ques-

tioned, eagerly and willing submitted themselves to Heaven's judgment in order to prove their innocence. For I only wish it were possible for me to walk bare-footed over glowing plow-shares, or hold a red-hot iron in my naked hands for the length of three pater-nosters, that I might show them to you, saying: "See — convince yourself— they are as white and unblem-ished as my integrity and my sincerity."

And now I will tell you who I really am. Perhaps you think you know already. This is not the first time that someone has been sent to work against you— nor will it be the last. Oh! my dear one, if there is one thing that makes me more miserable than our separa-tion, and the knowledge that your love for me is prob-ably dead, it is the thought of the terrible dangers that lurk all about you.

My Beloved, danger waits for you at every turn; in the very air you breathe, in the food you eat, in your sleep. There is peril in your telephone mouth-piece, in the electric wires in your house, under the rugs, in the soap with which you wash. I feel as though I must shriek aloud with terror and anxiety at the thought of the limitless possibilities that you are facing. How shall I be able to warn you in case this letter does not reach you? You may even destroy it unread, because it comes from me. If I could only give this paper a voice so that it could shout aloud its warning message.

Listen, oh! please listen to me. You have no idea of what he is capable of doing, that man for whom you are hunting. I cannot tell you who he is, for terrible as he is he is working for the right. But dear one, you must fear him. You are walking past a building under construction, a hoist breaks and you are crushed to death— an accident. You go to your rooms in the hotel elevator— it falls to the basement— an accident. Your car is crossing a street— another car dashes into it and you are killed . . . . the other driver was drunk. If he escapes with his life he is sentenced to prison, and escapes from the prison also— within the week.

The power of this great organization is beyond comprehension, my dearest. Chief Jason warned you — but not half enough. Don't be surprised that I know, for I am a member, and not an insignificant one, of that organization myself! I want to tell you everything I can. How I became a member. Everything but the name of the man who is the Chief of it all, and whose power is almost infinite, and the secrets that might bring about the hampering of its great work.

SPIES

My dear one, I have told you my real name. I *am* Sonia Nicolovena Baranikowa. Nicholas Gregorovitch Baranikowa was my father. A Nobleman. He was a great man with a heart of gold. He was a friend of the people. He fought for them as long as he lived. He was a thinker— far beyond Leo Tolstoy. My father did not wish to see the nobleman reduced to the rank of peasant, to become a labourer, a plodder, a stupid tiller of the soil. He wanted to see the peasant enlightened, freed from oppression, allowed to share his earnings, he wanted to see them with clean consciences, living clean lives, and able to enjoy life, taking pleasure in their work, and working for their pleasure; the women happy, pious without being superstitious,— strong and true like the colours of the windows in our cathedrals. It was my father's maxim that all injustice had its origin in misunderstanding.

Oh! my Beloved, I don't dare let myself write more about my father, or I will never stop. He was the idol of my childhood, and his ideals live within me now. And I have been working for them. I worshipped him. I loved him so much that when he died a part of me died too, and all that remained of me until you came into my life was a distorted shadow of my father's daughter; nothing remained of her but a deadly hatred, a vengeful, consuming hatred of his murderer.

I had a brother; Sascha Nicholaievitch, a handsome lad. You look like him when you smile. He was a fertile field for my father's teachings. His thoughts and ideas were the same as my father's, who had fired him with his own love for the people, made of him his most enthusiastic disciple.

My brother used to say, "I cannot visualize God other than with the face of my father."

One day they were both arrested. Ever since the early death of my mother I had kept house for them, and on this particular day the house was full of guests, whom I, dressed in my best clothes, was trying to entertain. I was really nothing but a child, and felt rather out of place among so many grown-ups. I was waiting nervously for my father's return. With every tick of the clock in the hall, my anxiety increased. I can still see that great clock before me, relentless moving its hands over its gem-studded face. A huge clock it was, very gorgeous, made of gold and lapis-lazuli, set with large semi-precious stones. On the quarter hours it played a soft little silvery tune, and on the hour deep chimes played our Tsar's national anthem.

Exactly one minute before eleven o'clock that terrible

159

night, my uncle took me by the hand and led me aside. I remember that his hand felt like a piece of ice, and that his lower lip trembled through his forced smile. He stopped near the big clock. The window next to it was open, and the evening breeze was blowing the silk curtains until they looked like fairy sails. He put his arms about me, and held me close. I was frightened. "Sonia Nicholovena," he said, and I marvelled that he could speak at all, he trembled so. "My dear one, I have terrible news for you. Control yourself— do not cry out. They have arrested your father and your brother. Under the orders of the Ochrana they are imprisoned in the Peter-Paul fortress. They have been charged with committing political crimes. No one is permitted to visit them; they are in solitary confinement. You have less than an hour in which to make your escape . . . . Dimitri Michailovitch Ochgolski doesn't waste any time."

I was stunned. Then a frantic desire to laugh swept over me. I remember the lights fading out of the brilliantly illuminated crystal chandeliers, and the vast room turning into an inky cavern— I could not see, I could not feel anything, I could only hear, clearly and harshly the noises of hurrying feet in the street, and the sound of a clock solemnly tolling the hour in a

distant church steeple, and then the great clock next
to me struck the full hour, its gong pealing eleven in
deep tones, and then the chimes ringing out the Tsar's
anthem. I listened to the end, then everything grew
black and blank.

I never saw my father or my brother again. They
were condemned to death and hastily executed, con-
victed of having plotted against their government.

I became desperately ill, and for a time it looked as
though I would lose my reason. But God showed me
no mercy— and I recovered. Ever since then I have
been searching for the man under whose direction my
father and brother were officially murdered— Dimitri
Michailovitch Ochgolski. I was little more than a
child when he condemned my dear ones to death, and
in the horror-stricken years that followed everything
in Russia changed so that any clues that might have
led me to him were wiped out. With friends and rela-
tives trying to help me to forget, I travelled all over
the world. But in vain. I could forget nothing. At
last I stumbled on a thread that offered me at least a
tiny lead— a chance of reaching my goal— the help of
the man for whom you are searching! I cannot tell
what I went through before I was able to make up my
mind to join the ranks of the spies working for this

Master-Spy. I would re-live that horrible time were I to write of it. So spare me that, Beloved.

I do not know how he came to find that I was searching for Ochgolski. He came to me while I was in Paris. "You are hunting for this man," he said, "and you have been told that he is probably dead. That is an error, or a deliberate lie. He is still living and active. He has changed his name, his vocation, his appearance, his very habits. I am prepared to put you in touch with him some day if you, in the meantime will join my forces."

It sounded simple enough, and yet I hesitated. But this man offered irresistible arguments. He laid his great scheme before me— the great end to which he is working. He showed me his book of plans, and convinced me of how closely related his ideals were to those of my dead father, though the methods he employed were far different. He won me over to the Cause.

He has not built up his great system of world espionage for personal gain. The fortune, the enormous wealth which is accruing from his organization's work, is carefully hoarded so that when the time is ripe, and when it has reached a sufficient amount, it may be poured forth in a golden torrent to sweep oppression from countless millions of the down-trodden.

In time, under his teaching I became his best spy. My dear one, as at a confessional, I kneel to you and strip the mask of pretense from my face. I have practised my profession with pleasure. Each successful day has seemed in some way to bring me nearer to the end I seek. I have plied my trade with enthusiasm — with the satisfaction born of hatred. I have enjoyed danger, and defeated it; I have courted adventure, and despised it. I've enjoyed trapping and duping people, and using them to attain my ends. I have held the fate of people and of nations in my hands, and rolled them about like marbles. That was what I was doing in that filthy hotel, playing with the fate of a nation.

Once I happened to see my own face in a mirror just after I had successfully completed an unusually dangerous negotiation, and I was horrified. I had never before known how scornful and bitter my eyes had become or how sinister my smile.

I received my orders to find out certain things from you. Orders from the very man you are hunting. I agreed to accept the mission. What were you to me then? Nothing but a number— a man whose craftiness was to dissolve before my own. I looked forward to pitting my wits against the best aide of the Chief of the Secret Service. I never planned anything more carefully than that murder farce at the Olympic, for I planned it all, Beloved, and never did I fail more miserably, before your kindness, your self-forgetfulness, your quick protection. Every action of yours, my dearest, from the moment I "fainted" in your arms was like a stab. I have suffered agonies for every untruth I have been obliged to utter. It was with the last vestige of self-respect that I fled from you.

I defied the Master. I refused to go on with his scheme. But I was not strong enough. And then a ray of hope came to me. He proposed that I try to win you over to his cause, and dictated the note that I sent you. I listened to him and obeyed, for it meant that at least I should see you once more. And in that second meeting I swear by the memory of my father there was not a single lie, not in the pressure of my hand, nor in the kisses from my lips, nor in my soul that poured to you from my eyes. My tongue alone had lied to you— would that I had bitten it out before the words passed my lips. But my love is not a lie. It is the only real thing left to me.

And at Danielli's, I received an order from the man you are seeking— he was there. I had to obey to safeguard you. God knows how you found that wretched hotel. That man I met there is a traitor from whom I bought his country's secrets. He tried to force his bestial attentions on me, that was what you saw. I would have killed him had I been armed.

What will happen now I don't know. Ever since I have shown that I would rather die than work against you any more, I have been kept a close prisoner. My home has been stripped bare. You must have looked for me there and found it so. What can we do?

In re-reading this letter I do not find that I have said one half of what I wanted to tell you, to make you believe. But you will believe me even now, my dearest one, you will— you will! My whole life seems to have crashed into ruins. I am not even permitted the chance to try and rebuild it.

But it is not for myself that I care. I am ill from worrying about you. How can I warn you sufficiently, convince you of the hopeless danger you are in? I must, and yet there is not even a window from this room out of which this note could go. I shall offer the guards my emerald ear-rings if they will take it to you, and if the Lord has any mercy you will receive it. Oh! my Beloved, believe my warnings and give up this futile and dangerous search. This man is too powerful. Remember how even the private secretary of your Chief was a member of this vast organization. Your very assistants may be ready to kill you, and only wait for their orders. My thoughts are driving me mad. Good-bye— with kisses on your lips, and eyes, and hands . . . . Sonia.

Within an hour after this letter had been placed in the hands of the bribed guard, it was returned to her, together with the ear-rings. Haghi's written comment was brief: "Noted. The guard is no longer able to appreciate jewelry!"

CHAPTER X

NUMBER 326 REPORTS

THERE was at least one thing of which Number 326 could boast. He was the only man, and probably would remain so for some time, whose appearance had ever so startled the Chief of the Secret Service as to make the latter drop his pipe from his mouth.

"Great Heavens!" ejaculated Miles Jason, staring at his aide, "what has happened to you?"

He might well ask the question, for this hollow-eyed, haggard man who stood before him bore little resemblance to the ever calm and imperturbable Number 326.

He ignored his Chief's inquiry. "I have found a clue," he said, moistening his dry lips.

"Yes— yes, boy— fine, fine—!! But what has happened to you?"

"Nothing—," replied Number 326 almost sullenly. "I've found a clue, that's all."

"Hmm!— I see. . . ." Miles Jason spoke slowly, without moving his eyes from the young man. He packed the bowl of his pipe, and swore irritably when he found it too tight. "Hmm!" he grunted, after a long contemplation, "you look a damned sight less like a man who has found something than one who has lost something— something which he needs sorely— his commonsense, his brains and— his Chief's confidence!"

Number 326 flushed scarlet.

"I beg your pardon, Sir! Just what do you mean, Mr. Jason?"

"By the gods," roared the Chief, "I'm glad to see that you still have enough spunk to be insulted." He fumbled for his great spectacles without which he could not see anything nearer than three feet, and clapped them on. "Just what do I mean," he continued, pounding his fist on the desk, "I'll tell you!"

He sprang from his chair, and seizing Number 326 by the shoulders, peered closely into his face. "Who is the damned woman?" he shouted.

Number 326 wrenched himself away, and at his expression, Miles Jason felt himself choke back the words he was about to speak, and sought refuge in shaking his head in sincere regret.

"I'd really like to know," he muttered, moodily returning to his chair, "what the Lord Almighty had in mind when he deprived a perfectly good man of a perfectly good rib to create thereof that catastrophe, Eve." He leaned forward over the desk, and spoke gently to Number 326 who had dropped wearily into the chair on the far side. "Tell me all about it, boy."

The young man drew a deep breath, seemed about to answer, but found no words. He sank his drawn, ashen face into his hands. "I've stumbled on a clue," he repeated dully. Then, with a quick shake of his head, he raised it, and looked his Chief squarely in the eyes— those sympathetic, choleric eyes.

"Forgive me, Chief— don't lose your temper. Forgive me. You are right— I've been a hopeless fool! I don't know how much has been reported to you, but I've been even more of an idiot than you can suspect. I suppose every one has to learn by experience, and to pay for that . . . . God knows I've paid for mine. But it *is* paid for— and the account is closed. You need not retract your confidence.

"Do you know a Dr. Matsumoto?" he asked suddenly.

"As well as anyone can know an Oriental," answered Jason grimly.

"Is he one of our opponents, or an ally?"

The Chief grunted. "Why the good Lord made them, He only knows, and He only knows what goes on behind the masks they call faces. Just at present the East wind is blowing favourably; how long it will last *I* don't presume to foretell. This Dr. Matsumoto is here as a special ambassador from his nation. That there is to be an important treaty signed shortly is common knowledge, but where and when is not known." His face suddenly set sternly. "Our friend— this Master Mind— is going to make it his business to find out, however. I am as sure of that as that God made little apples. That's his *business*. That's why I sent for you in a hurry. He knows I did, and he staged that play at the Olympic as the first move against you. Now this Dr. Matsumoto, to go back to your question, must keep that treaty out of his hands, so for the time being at least he's on our side."

"Would you trust him, Chief— trust his word?"

"He's 90% gentleman, boy."

"Sufficient, Chief. Now listen."

To Miles Jason it was like watching a man tear open a terrible wound, and brutally cleanse it. For

Number 326 did not spare himself in his recital of all that had happened since, as the tramp, he had left this office— it seemed so many ages ago.

".... and when my head had cleared enough, and my brain would function, I found that hotel from which she had fled. It must have been the scoundrel's rat-hole, for although he had on a dress-shirt and trousers he was wearing a silk dressing-gown.

"When I found it, he had gone— disappeared entirely— departed for good apparently, for he left nothing behind not even a mail address. I searched the hole, from the vermin-infested walls to the cracks in the ceiling— sifted the ashes in the stove, examined light-bulbs and switches— everything— for finger-prints. Not a trace of anything— he's no beginner.

"But he couldn't take away my memory of his face. I could recognize him anywhere— him or his picture— smug, slimy, insinuating— like a cheap perfume. And I'm going to find him, Chief, and work up from him.

"You warned me of danger, but they didn't try to put me out of the way. They did much worse— they made a fool out of me. And it's not very flattering to be turned into a complete fool, such a blind— trusting — fool. . . . . .

"That woman—," he snapped, "I *know* now without a shadow of doubt serves the same master as Vincent did— the man we want!"

Chief Jason had sat silent and motionless. This kindly, explosive, gentle and seemingly unreasonable man had, from long experience, learned the value of listening. Throughout the recital of Number 326, he had sat, mouthing the stem of his pipe, rolling his jaw strangely like a sullen cow chewing its cud.

As Number 326 ended, he pointed toward a cabinet on the far side of the office. "Sixth book— second row— bring it here. Every suspect— look 'em over."

Number 326 scrutinized the great collections of photographs. Many of them were enlargements of parts of tiny snapshots, the subjects caught often in ridiculous poses, but all were sufficient for identification of the originals. Rapidly, he turned page after page— why, there were scores!—

The Chief watched him, and saw that Number 326 was hunting, not with the impersonal zeal of the professional, but with the eagerness of a man bent on personal revenge.

Suddenly, Number 326 stiffened like a pointing dog. His hand trembled as it held the page he had just turned, and it was an appreciable moment before he

spoke. "This is the man, Chief," he said calmly, the
flame in his eyes belying the tone of his voice.

Jason avoided the young man's eyes— they troubled
him— and looked at the photograph.

"Jellusic!" he muttered. "Jellusic— Colonel of the
Headquarters Staff of— hmmmm! he's not a
cheap buy— extravagant tastes— expensive habits—
women—"

He lifted the phone. "Supervisor's office— yes—
Number 68— yes— yes— Yes— bring report number R/G 68,999 Q.M.J. . . . . Yes—Jason talking."

Number 68 responded with amazing celerity. He
was a mild unobtrusive little man, with keen twinkling
eyes. It was easy to imagine him flattening invisibly
against a wall, or melting into a corner, leaving nothing visible but those eyes. And though the ears
might not show, there was a certain alertness about
them that indicated an ability to catch most of what
might be going on. He had never been known
to make a written note, and had never been known to
make an erroneous statement of fact. His oral reports— he invariably refused to make a written one—
on the cases to which he had been detailed were made
like the automaton that he was— never an inflection of
the voice— never a change of tone.

"Mirko Jellusic— No. 386923/ Dept. R/G Div. 68,999 Q.M.J.

"Under observation four months— travels back and forth from the Balkans with certain regularity. Confirmed gambler— fond of women— no taste or discrimination— generous— talks too much. Boasts about his conquests. His latest mistress. . . . . ."

A choking sound from the throat of Number 326 interrupted him. He turned his quick beady eyes upon the young man, evidently annoyed at this break in the regularity of his routine.

"Go on— go on!" cried Number 326. His hands were clenched till the knuckles showed white. Even Chief Jason gripped the arms of his chair.

"Are you questioning my report, sir?" snapped Number 68 indignantly.

"Go on with it," growled the Chief.

". . . . his latest mistress was Magda Clarence, long distance telephone operator, station. . . . . ."

But again his mechanical recital was broken into by a cry from Number 326. Number 68 stared in astonishment at the young man, whose face was glowing with a great joy, and glanced from him to the Chief, to meet with even a greater amazement, for the latter had tossed his arms into the air and dropped

174

back in his chair with a whoop of delight. Then his
face clouded again. Number 68 thought he heard him
mutter: "The better she is, the worse for him."

Having waited, to see if there were to be any
further interruptions, the supervisor continued: "Exactly forty-six hours ago, Mirko Jellusic called for
three letters at the general delivery window No. 96. He
wrote a cipher under which they were evidently held.
He wrote with his own fountain-pen. He was handed
the letters without question. After he had left the building, I identified myself, and secured the paper. It was
blank. The writing had faded— evidently a special
ink. It has been impossible for our chemists to bring
it back.

"For two days, Mirko Jellusic occupied a room
at. . . . . ."

"We know that," broke in the Chief, "what else?"

Number 68 restrained his indignation. "That
room," he continued "was searched with remarkable
thoroughness between 4.30 and 6.30 this morning by
Number 326. Without result. Mirko Jellusic left this
morning on his way to the Balkans at 4.02 A.M."

"Number 68," cried Number 326, "you are great!
Thanks more than I can say. Chief, with your permission I'm going to follow that rat. He'll make con-

nections with the Orient Express, and in a plane I can pick him up at any of a dozen cities."

The Chief was already at the telephone: "Get me the Aero-Lloyd," he ordered. "How soon can you start?"

"I'm ready now," replied Number 326. "I can phone Franz to meet me at the flying-field with my luggage."

The phone rang, and at a motion from the Chief, Number 68 answered.

"Yes? . . . . One seat?" he questioned, extending his index finger.

"Certainly— one seat," replied Number 326.

"One seat immediate—"

"But I must see Dr. Matsumoto before I go," Number 326 suddenly remembered. "I owe him that much consideration, Chief."

"Plane No. 182, seat 6. Leaving in forty-five minutes," called Number 68 from the telephone.

Number 326 hurriedly shook Jason's hand, waved at Number 68, whose orderly and methodical soul was disturbed by this rushing about on the moment, instead of moving along well planned lines, and tore out the door.

Eight minutes later, he rang the bell at the address

given him by his Oriental friend. Dr. Matsumoto himself opened the door. He seemed genuinely glad to see Number 326. He glanced knowingly at the face of his visitor, a face from which the pallor of poison, madness and fatigue had faded, to give way to a flush of eager hurry. "You are better," he said. "It is marvellous— this recuperation of youth."

He ushered his guest into a small, simply furnished room adjoining the one where he had been working.

Kitty, the small waif, had been lying on a cushion beside him, cleaning his pipes. As soon as the doctor had left the room, she sprang to her feet with the speed and silence of a cat. She was dressed from head to foot in an elaborate kimono, so soft that there was never a rustle to it, and her stockinged feet moved across the floor without a sound. She kept a pipe in her hand, as she slipped to the door to listen.

Number 326 was speaking rapidly. He was voicing his gratitude for the timely assistance and counsel of this gentle stranger— and was explaining his hurry. The eyes of the Oriental lighted with hope, as he heard the reason for that haste, and he spoke an age-old "benediction" as the young man gripped his hand and sped away.

Kitty listened just long enough. Quickly stepping

177

to the farther wall, she tapped intermittently upon the magnificent temple-banner that draped it— a portrayal of Buddha's descent to the lower regions. Behind the wall, concealed so that even the removal of the tapestry would not disclose it, was the microphone which transmitted to Haghi's headquarters the message which she rapped out:

"Number 326 following Jellusic leaves by plane Number 182."

When Dr. Matsumoto returned to his study, he found Kitty as he had left her, industriously cleaning his pipes. The look of adoration that she gave him was unbelievable in its beautiful innocence. He could have stroked her hair from where he seated himself— that marvellous silken hair that shone so incongruously against her Oriental costume, but he resisted the temptation, and merely returned her smile— the smile of a happy child, looking up to a god who has rescued her and given her warmth and happiness. He did reach down, however, and adjust the kimono, which was slipping from her exquisite shoulder. "The cold-blooded fish!" muttered the innocent "child."

Kitty's report shot before Haghi from the chute on his desk. He showed no sign of discomposure or even

178

of annoyance, except a slight contraction of the brows shadowing those imperturbable eyes. It was as if a gentleman farmer had learned of the loss of, not a prize-winner, but a good producing cow. A minor source of supply cut off.

"It would seem," he said to himself, "as if the good Colonel had outlived his usefulness."

His eyes narrowed, and then closed. Petra, standing behind him, handed him in silence one cigarette after another. The electric clock ticked away the minutes.

Haghi dropped to the floor a half-finished cigarette. He reached for the telephone.

"Take a message to War Department 473, M.S.H. address R. 590. 'Report Jellusic.' "

Petra had in her hand the cigarette for which he reached.

CHAPTER XI

SENTENCED

THE Minister of War was a man who abhorred nothing so much as the showing of emotions— what place could emotions hold in the breast of a man whose orders made or ruined the lives of thousands? He must be as ruthless and as hard as the god of the ancient Scriptures, or as relentless as Baal. He was tremendously impressed with the importance of his position, and did not realize that the only reason the European Powers paid any attention to his pocket-handkerchief of a country was because it was the tiny posterngate that could admit them to things worth while.

The Minister ridiculed everything which emphasized his rank, and he did it so cleverly that he almost believed it himself. Certainly those of his aides who were without a sense of humour believed without reservation in his unselfish devotion to his country. His adjutant was one who did not possess that saving grace;

he not only believed and respected the Minister, but he believed and respected the easily bought traitors that were in power— his liege lords! the scum that have, for generations, made the Balkans the cess-pool of Europe— the breeding-place of the worst of all diseases — War.

As white as his own ever-immaculate gloves, the adjutant entered the office of his chief. He was too disturbed to let even the sight of the disorderly desk disturb further his orderly soul. A samovar, coffee-cups, ash-trays, flasks of vodka, contracts and pacts and treaties were all jumbled into a sordid disorder.

The Minister, and the two Generals in his company, were in the most genial frame of mind. Had the Adjutant been less disturbed he might have noted that the vodka flasks were almost empty.

"What can I do for you, old man?" asked the Minister. "Have a drink." The Adjutant shuddered.

"Thanks, no,— Your Excellency."

"Well then I'll have to drink for you. Here's to you."

But he did not drink. He looked up, as he spoke, saw the face of his aide— and his glass remained in mid-air.

"What's wrong, sir," he demanded angrily, smashing the glass down on the table. "Are you venturing to criticize me?"

The Adjutant glanced significantly at the two Generals, who were leaning forward in their chairs. The Minister spoke with alcoholic sharpness. "What's the matter with you— talk!"

The Adjutant snapped to attention.

"Your Excellency, Col. Malakoi respectfully requests an immediate audience with you, to discuss a matter of vital importance. I transmit his urgent request that the audience be private."

The Minister of War gnawed his bristling white moustache. He frowned, and lifting his glass slowly, drained it, without removing his eyes from his adjutant's face.

"You know what he wants to talk about, don't you?"

"Yes, your Excellency."

"Then why don't you tell me what it's all about?"

"I respectfully beg of your Excellency," the Adjutant replied desperately— his lips were grey— "to receive the report from Col. Malakoi yourself, and— alone!"

"I'm damned at your impertinence, sir," roared the Minister. "Are you to tell me, the Minister of War, to usher out my Chief of Staff and my Chief of Ordnance, because a miserable colonel wants to talk to me. You forget yourself, sir! Tell Malakoi to come in." He poured himself another drink, first into his glass and then into his throat, and sat back in complete self-satisfaction.

Colonel Malakoi entered. The man was evidently finding it difficult to maintain his composure. He saluted firmly and respectfully, but his teeth were gritted to keep his mouth from quivering.

"Well, Malakoi," questioned the Minister, "what is it that's so important? Something pretty, I'll bet."

"Yes, your Excellency, it is as your Excellency wishes."

"Well, what is it?" roared the Minister.

The colonel saluted again: "I regret to report that I have received definite advice from Section A of the Bureau of Investigation that they have discovered that a traitor has been selling military secrets of our country, and that they have now found who he is."

In the intense silence that followed, the room crackled with tension. Not a man moved. All eyes hung on Malakoi's lips.

"Well— well—!" gasped the Minister, "go on, man! Who is it— who is it?"

Malakoi gulped twice before he could answer. Then
he drew himself to his full height in rigid salute.

"Colonel Mirko Jellusic, of the General Staff, and
special aide to your Excellency!"

The Minister of War slumped so suddenly backward that the officers, who had been stunned by Malakoi's statement, sprang to life and to assist him. He
shook away their help. His face flushed, then purpled,
and great beads of sweat broke out upon his forehead.
His eyes bulged, and his fists crashed down on the table,
sending the glasses to the floor.

"Are you mad, sir? Are you . . . . Are you . . . .
Damn it man, do you know that Colonel Jellusic is to
be my son-in-law?"

Colonel Malakoi held his rigid position.

. The Minister sank back again, and lifted a trembling hand in a silent gesture that conveyed more of
an apology than any spoken word could have done.
The silence became almost unbearable.

At last the Minister raised his head, and turned his
blood-shot eyes upon the bearer of this terrible report.
The question upon his face was so clear that Col.
Malakoi replied as though to a spoken query.

"Unfortunately, your Excellency, there is no room
for doubt; there is irrefutable proof."

"We can not afford to have either an arrest or a scandal."

SENTENCED

"I must see the proof," muttered the Minister, hoarsely.

Colonel Malakoi reached to the pocket of his tunic, and laid upon the table before the Minister a batch of papers. Those who dared to watch saw the face of their commander turn a leaden grey. He raised his head at the end of his examination.

"Gentlemen," he said calmly, in a voice they did not recognize, "there is no doubt of the truth of this accusation. And from what source, Colonel Malakoi, did this information reach the bureau?"

"That, your Excellency, we could not trace. A telephone call that gave us definite information— information that we could not disregard— an act of vengeance."

"Enough!" said the Minister. He rose with an effort that sent the blood back to the face that had paled to the colour of ashes as he had turned over the damning evidence in the papers before him. Straight and with head erect, he stood— possibly for the first time a real commander.

"Gentlemen—" the officers had never suspected that this tone could come from the throat of their genial Minister, "gentlemen, this man Jellusic must be— removed!"

"Your Excellency," ventured the Adjutant, in a voice pitched high in his excitement, "to arrest Colonel Jellusic would start an impossible scandal."

The Minister glared fiercely at the white faced speaker, and crashed his knuckles on the table: "I have not mentioned arrest! There can be no arrest— nor any scandal! I trust I make myself clear, gentlemen!" . . . . his eyes questioned one after the other. Death-like silence reigned. He continued: "This— this— affair must be cleared before the day is over. You know at what time the Express is due, as well as the address of— this man. Is there anything further for me to say, gentlemen?"

As the two officers saluted, wheeled and left the room, the Minister glanced down at the table, and the evidence of the happy conviviality of so short a time ago— his knees seemed to give way beneath him, and he sank into his chair, his chin upon his breast. His eyes closed. The two generals tip-toed from the room.

CHAPTER XII

"AS YE SOW"

THE train pulled into the station. Mirko Jellusic,
rousing himself from the comfort of a pleasant journey
and a compartment all to himself, and assisted by a
well-tipped porter, stepped from the train almost as
soon as it had stopped. He had changed from his
travelling tweeds into his uniform, and, having noted
his appearance in the mirror of the compartment, was
in an unusually good humour. As he left the seat in
the train, he lifted from the table before him an envelope which he had been regarding with much satisfaction, and for many miles. As the porter took his
luggage, and searched for a vacant taxi, Colonel Jellusic sought the nearest mail box. A blind man,
tapping his way with his cane, and led by a little dog,
stumbled against him; the dog wound the leash about
his legs. Jellusic was about to resent the incident
when he saw the infirmity of the man. He stopped,

unwound the leash, and slipped some money into the hand of the dog's owner. Then, turning to the mailbox, he dropped in the bulky letter which the "blind" man had seen most plainly was addressed to "Opernball 13—General Delivery."

Mirko Jellusic drove on home. He was feeling gloriously stimulated and exhilarated as though he had been drinking excellent, long-promised champagne. He was well pleased with life, both in particular and in general— and very much pleased with himself. He was looking forward toward pleasing a pleasant woman, and he hummed a sentimental tune as he leaned back in the taxi.

Suddenly it occurred to him that his striker had not been at the station to meet him. The lazy scoundrel! But, then, Jellusic smiled— probably playing around with some woman, and had forgotten. Well, he was young— only a lad— and boys will be boys— and hadn't he done the same thing himself. . . . . .

The chauffeur of the taxi carried the trunk into the foyer, and received such a tip that he was unable to do anything for the remainder of the day but absorb liquor.

Colonel Jellusic, successful in his profession, successful with the ladies, successful in his "speculations," unfortunate only in gambling, whistled cheerfully as he walked up the stairs to his rooms. Fortunate, that he had his keys— for that good-for-nothing was not even at home! Well. . . . ? Jellusic smiled indulgently as he unlocked the door, and swung it open. He was in no mood to be harsh. Groping for the switch, he turned on the lights, and stepped back quickly— but not quickly enough. A man had leaped between him and the door, barring his way. He stared at the intruder— it was the Adjutant, the aide of the Minister of War. Dully, he swung about, and faced the other figure who stood rigid in the centre of the apartment: Colonel Malakoi!

For a full minute— sixty interminable seconds— there was a silence that could almost be heard, then the voice of Colonel Malakoi:

"I can see that it is true— Mister Jellusic!"

The word struck him like a bullet, and he staggered as if physically wounded, *"Mister*—MISTER!"

The game was up. . . . *"Mister!"*

"It *is* true," he answered. "Gentlemen, I submit to your arrest."

There was a horrible silence. At last, moistening his lips, Colonel Malakoi spoke:

"The honour of the country and of the army are at stake, Mr. Jellusic— There will be *no arrest!*"

For an instant, the condemned man stared in bewilderment— and then understanding came to him. Hesitatingly, as if he wondered whether he still had the right to do so, he stumbled to a chair, and fell into it. He buried his head in his arms. The two officers made no movement or sign.

At last he raised his head. "May I write a few letters, gentlemen?"

"No, Mr. Jellusic."

"Why, no— of course not," Jellusic laughed. "People who have . . . . people who are fortunate enough to— to have *accidents* don't write farewell letters . . . . no . . . . of course not. . . . . ."

He dropped into the utter blackness of it all— to stop— not to see— not to hear— not to feel— to die— to what—? . . . . And by his own hand. . . . . . !

"If you have any reasonable last request to make, Mr. Jellusic—" came the voice of Colonel Malakoi.

"I have," the man replied quietly, with a sudden composure. He looked at the white faces of the two officers, and drawing himself up to his full height, he continued: "Gentlemen, my striker has absented himself, apparently for the night. He takes care of my.

fire-arms. I feel that I may be greatly in need of a pistol or revolver to-night. If one of you would be so good. . . . ?"

Colonel Malakoi laid upon the table his service revolver, and, turning without a word, walked to the door which the Adjutant had opened.

Outside, they waited, avoiding each other's eyes. The moments quickened like the blood that dripped from the Colonel's lip where he had bitten it, and like the sweat that broke upon the Adjutant's forehead—and then the very seconds extended into eternity in that nerve-racking silence. The shot crashed through the unearthly stillness, muffling the sound of the falling body— and then— silence.

Simultaneously, the two officers stiffened to attention, and saluted. They were not saluting the dead man beyond the door— they were paying their respects to the second of the two Great Mysteries.

CHAPTER XIII

THE PACKAGE IN THE MAIL

A DEPRESSING foggy twilight shrouded the landing field, as Number 326 climbed out of the plane. The flickering lights accentuated, rather than dispelled, the gloom. A man moved out from the crowd of people meeting friends, porters, and employees of the company, and stumbling, fell against Number 326. The latter did not stop, but catching his balance walked on. "I beg your pardon, sir," apologized the stranger, and then, in a quick undertone: "were you by any chance born on the third day of February at 6:00 o'clock?"

"Do you know the wedding day of your grandparents?" questioned Number 326, without turning his head.

"Fortunately, it was the 18th of June."

"Fine!" said Number 326. "I hope you've got a car here— I'm in a great hurry."

By this time, they were leaving the field, and were safely out of ear-shot of anyone who had seen the meeting. "Not so great a hurry as you think, comrade," replied the man. "You've not seen the news."

Number 326 stopped short. He felt instinctively that something had occurred to upset his plans— that some unseen hand had reached from the shadows and robbed him.

His companion, whom Number 326 knew now as a fellow worker— Number 187, extended a newspaper. Under the nearest street-light it was possible to read the following item:

"Word has just been received of the death of Colonel Mirko Jellusic of the Headquarters General Staff, upon his return home from a leave of absence. The Colonel was striken in his rooms by a sudden and fatal attack of heart-failure. The unexpected death of this capable officer, who was respected and esteemed alike by his superiors and his men, has brought to a premature close a career of great promise. His demise is a severe blow to the Service."

Number 326 caught his breath. He read and re-read the article. A sense of hot indignation was his first emotion; anger that his legitimate prey had been snatched from him. The man was dead, and he could never have the satisfaction of shaking from that vile mouth the answers that would tell of the woman and the master who ruled them. Again he re-read the article, and something in the very brevity of it seemed to give it the lie. There was something here to be followed up. He folded the paper and pocketed it.

"You are right," he said to his companion, "for the moment I am no longer in a hurry. Will you please let me have your full report."

"I waited for him, according to orders, at the railroad station. I had no difficulty in recognizing him—the telephoto was excellent, and his moustache hasn't its duplicate in Europe. He was in uniform, and made no effort to conceal his movements. He appeared absolutely self-assured and carefree. I was made up as a blind man, and had every chance to get a good look at him. He carried a thick letter in his hand which he mailed at the nearest box. But before he had reached this, I had stumbled against him, and Dandy, my little dog, had wound the leash about his legs. As he stooped to free himself with a good-natured laugh, I could see clearly the address on the envelope in his hand. It was: "Opernball 13, General Delivery."

Number 187 found his arm in a grasp of steel. Number 326 was rushing him toward his car. "Now we *are* in a hurry! That address may be worth its weight in gold. Drive like hell, man, to the central post-office."

They shot into the night, splashing through the wet streets at frantic speed. They arrived at the postal building just four minutes before closing time. As they tore into the doorway, a shabbily dressed man shuffled in directly behind them. He was splashed with mud from head to foot, like a trunk or a bag that has been carried on the rear of a car in bad weather. He went to the writing booths as if to write a telegram. He seemed to have difficulty. Passing from booth to booth, he grumbled at the conditions of the pens in each one, as he snapped and broke the points in all of them, and the lack of pencils even, as he slipped them into his own pocket. At the last booth he halted, and wrote.

Number 326 and his companion paid no attention to this grumbling individual, for they were eager upon their own business. With a forced air of assurance, Number 326 went directly to the General Delivery window, and in a rather hoarse voice, hoarse from the excitement he could barely control, asked for the mail held under the cipher "Opernball 13." Neither of the two men drew a breath until the taciturn clerk returned from the depths of the post-office and silently handed them a letter. "That's the one," whispered Number 187.

Number 326 stepped back from the window, and leaned suddenly against the wall of the office. He was indignant at his weakness— still weak. And yet he stared over the top of the letter in his hand and into space— seeing the image of a man— a man in a dress-shirt and silk dressing-gown— framed in a doorway— a dirty yellow light shining on his face. And the face distorted— transparent— the sordid leer twisted into a horrible grin— the grin of a Death's head; it nodded— beckoned to him. . . . . .

He gulped, and hurriedly tore open the envelope, nearly destroying it in his vehemence.

It contained nothing but a bundle of bank-notes— not a single written word— not a single identifying mark! Their great find was useless!

Number 326 said nothing. Mechanically he undid the package of notes, and ran them though— twenty thousand pounds sterling, a fortune!

Suddenly, Number 326 leaped for the writing booths, in his eagerness nearly knocking down the bespotted individual who was still struggling with his message. The man shrank back, and relinquished his place at this last desk, the only one where there remained a pen or a pencil or even telegraph blanks.

Number 326 wrote, not even troubling to translate his message into cipher: "General Delivery, Box 30 . . . . Find at once to whom Bank notes in sequence x1003480 to x1003499 thousand pounds each were issued. Returning next plane must have information on arrival. 326."

As the two Secret Service men left the office, the shabby individual emerged from his retreat in the corner where he had stepped, and, going straight to the desk on which Number 326 had written his message, deftly lifted up the blotter and revealed a piece of carbon paper beneath it. The method had been successful. None too clear, and yet quite legible, there was the copy of the message.

He left the building quickly, and hurried to the next nearest telephone station. "I want a long distance call— very urgent," he announced, and anticipated the operator's hesitation at complying to such a request from such an obviously poverty-stricken tramp, by reaching into his pocket and laying a large bill on the desk.

Haghi sat in his hidden office, alone, save for the ever-present Petra behind him.

He was silently contemplating two papers that lay before him. One, in a shaky trembling hand, but still recognizable as the writing of the unfortunate Lady Elinore Leslane, he knew by heart: "The treaty will be signed. . . ." The refusal of Ah Hi to supply her with any of the horrid drug which now meant more to her than her life or her honour, had swept aside her last thought of resisting. She had delivered her information.

The other paper was a hastily pencilled message:

"Elinore Leslane jumped from her window ten minutes ago. Morrier."

"Well," said Haghi, at last, "Ah Hi has lost another good customer."

His private phone rang; it was long distance: the report of the telegram sent by Number 326.

CHAPTER XIV

THE TREATY

In a quiet room, in a building, unostentatious despite the fact that it was the embassy of a great nation, two men sat at a table. Surrounding them were several others, motionless, standing at military attention.

The seated men reached for the pens that lay before them and the stillness of the room was broken by the scratch of the signatures that made valid in those few seconds the agreement between two great empires— that ended the years of unceasing diplomatic effort— and wrote *finis* to the legal efforts of a generation.

The face of Sir Roger Leslane, as he put down his pen, was that of an exhausted victor in a long race— drawn and white— but it held also the great relief that comes with the knowledge that the effort is over.

The face of his *vis-à-vis* was like an Oriental mask,— serenely smiling, betraying the tenseness of the situation only by the slightest quivering of his contracted jaw muscles.

The documents were exchanged, hands were clasped, and the pungent odor of sealing wax permeated the room.

As Sir Roger Leslane rose from his chair, he rose with the knowledge that this treaty just signed had secured for the country he represented extraordinary advantages, but whenever he had dealt with Orientals, he had always left an interview with a strange feeling that even greater advantages had been obtained by the other side. In this case, however, he felt that he could not be wrong, provided that the terms of the treaty did not become common news of the day. He glanced about the room, as he rose. There were his aides, the Oriental envoy, and his special envoy, Dr. Matsumoto, and Chief of the Secret Service, Miles Jason. Surely no leak here.

He was bowing his leave, when a commotion was heard outside the door. Excited voices spoke loudly— the door-handle rattled— there was a sound of a struggle— and the door burst open to admit the terror-stricken valet of Sir Roger, followed by a member of his diplomatic corps. The gasping sentences of the valet blanched the face of the successful statesman, and tore from him the self-satisfaction of his just accomplished achievement. He staggered to the door, assisted by the valet.

Miles Jason reached suddenly for the arm of the man who had entered with the valet. "Is that true?" he snapped, "was it suicide? Answer, man, I'm Chief Jason."

The man bowed his head in assent.

The Chief rushed from the room without even the courtesy of a bow. The envoy allowed his slanting eyes to turn for a moment and therefore did not see the unoriental emotion that for a fleeting instant marked his compatriot's face.

They were now alone— the envoy and Dr. Matsumoto. As one, they rose, and moved to the door. Although everything had been said that there was need to say, each seemed to hesitate, waiting for some final word. The Envoy reached for the door-knob, but Dr. Matsumoto had anticipated his action; yet he did not turn the handle.

The Envoy, a descendant of a race of Samurai, whose ancestry could be traced back for thousands of years, spoke apologetically— almost diffidently, as an officer in war-time might speak to a volunteer for an almost hopeless mission.

"Any mention of your sense of responsibility," he said— "any reference to the trust placed in you, would be a reflection upon your ability, your honour and your patriotism. You will then forgive me for saying that I envy the great honour that has been granted you, Dr. Matsumoto, in being chosen to safeguard the transmission of this treaty!"

"Your Excellency," replied Dr. Matsumoto quietly, but with a ring of steel in his voice, "the treaty will reach the august hands of our Emperor with the seals intact, or the lives of four loyal subjects will lie, remorseful, at his feet."

The Envoy did not reply— he bowed in deep salutation, and passed through the door that Dr. Matsumoto held open for him. Even then, the last word seemed to have been left unsaid.

Dr. Matsumoto returned to the table where but a few minutes ago had been signed the paper that still lay upon it. He seated himself, and, taking a small key from his watch-chain unlocked the center drawer. He took from it three envelopes, long and narrow and so alike that only microscopic examination could have shown any difference between them— the texture and the twists of the strings that tied them were identical— the paper showed the same water-marks, each in the same place— and even the seals of red wax that held the strings had been kept to a marvellous similarity. The three envelopes were alike in weight to the fraction of an ounce. . . . They were uninscribed.

Dr. Matsumoto placed them carefully before him on the great table. As he did so, he pushed aside a Japanese newspaper which was lying folded on the desk. He touched an electric button, leaned back, and waited.

A few seconds later, the dark panelling of the wall facing him opened slowly and silently. Three men entered. They were shabbily clothed in the costumes of wretched coolies— their faces were evil. Dr. Matsumoto rose and bowed with deference, for he was greeting not only the scions of three noble houses, but three men to whom their country was all.

Each replied to the salutation with a dignified obeisance. They ranged themselves opposite the silent figure, as the Doctor sank back in the chair behind the table.

"My Lords . . . . Gentlemen," Matsumoto corrected himself quickly, "gentlemen, you see before you there on the table three envelopes. One of these should contain the most important State document to which a representative of your country has affixed his signature in

generations. Each of you will take one of these envelopes, and each will travel by a different route. The
man who does not deliver this treaty envelope into the
hands of his Emperor, with seals unbroken, is not fit
to live as subject to our Divine Ruler."

He handed each man one of the envelopes, and each
concealed it in his shabby garments. There was no
further spoken word. The three bowed deeply, and
again Doctor Matsumoto rose and bowed in humble
obeisance to silent courage. He knew that he was
sending these men to their deaths— and he knew that
they knew this, also, and yet had accepted their com-
missions with pride.

For a moment, after the door had closed behind the
three condemned men, Dr. Matsumoto stood with
bent head; then, picking up the folded newspaper which
lay upon the desk, he tucked it carelessly under his
arm and started for his home.

That newspaper contained, unwrapped, unsealed, un-
protected save by the very lack of concealment and care
with which it was carried, the treaty which had just
been signed!

Dr. Matsumoto entered his own house like a thief.
He knew only too well in his heart the reason for his
silence— lack of courage. He could not bear the

thought of saying good-bye to Kitty. He was about to steal away from these rooms, leaving behind the only human being in this city of millions of inhabitants to whom his thoughts had turned with real affection. . . . He had been moved by the distress of Number 326, yes, but that had been different. For days, he had been carrying around, hidden in absurd ways the tickets for this trip. In two hours, the sleeper would be carrying him away from this city and the exquisite little waif who within these short hours had crept so into his great heart.

It was perhaps his own preoccupation— his concentration on the tiny noises he himself was making that prevented him from noticing the almost inaudible tapping of Kitty's message to the sinister cripple sitting in his invalid's chair, listening intently through a pair of ear-phones.

Dr. Matsumoto's mind was fully made up. He would sneak away, and leave a farewell letter behind— a letter making the girl the mistress of this house, and providing against her every want. Never again should she be obliged to huddle shivering and drenched to the skin in a rain-soaked doorway rather than return to the drunken beatings of her parents. Perhaps at some later time he could send for her— but now it was impossible to take her with him. The treaty, and that alone, was his duty.

He crept silently to his bedroom door. The unshaded windows were already admitting a grey light of dawn. He drew the curtains before switching on the electric bulbs. From a shelf in the wardrobe, he drew out a heavy valise, put it on the table, and placed the newspaper containing the treaty in the locked pocket of the lid. He hurriedly threw in the clothes necessary for his journey, and with the placing of each garment, the pain in his heart seemed to increase. "Little Plum-blossom," he thought— "little white peony— farewell!"

A faint sound, hardly more than the rustle of a leaf, startled him. He leaned against the table, trying to hide the half-packed valise, and smiled sadly as the girl opened the door to stop, framed in the hangings. She was clad in the robes of a Japanese maiden, and with eyes raised expectantly awaited the man's permission to enter— an exquisite picture of tender, shy beauty. She must have heard him, he thought, despite his efforts to be silent, and knowing how he invariably liked a final cup of tea at bedtime, had arisen, dressed herself carefully in his native costume, even taking the trouble to drape the *obi* elaborately, and prepare it for him. She held in her hand a scarlet lacquer tray on which steamed a fragile bowl of green tea. Although the smile remained on her lips, her eyes opened in startled amazement.

"Kitty," said the doctor, in gentle reproof, "why aren't you fast asleep?"

She stared at him wildly, and then her eyes leaped from him to the open portmanteau. The tray slipped from her hand, and the fragile porcelain cup shattered on the floor. "You are going away— you are going to leave me," she whispered, and swaying, she would have fallen had not the man caught her as she tottered forward. He uttered a sharp exclamation as she slumped into his arms, pulling one hand back quickly. The brooch from her throat dropped to the floor. She seized his wrist: "Did it scratch you— did it scratch you?" she cried, and covered the wrist with affectionate and remorseful kisses.

Then the petty tragedy swept before the flood of the greater. "You are going away," she cried again. "No— no! You must not!"

He tried to reason with her— what was he saying? Empty words— over and over again— his head wasn't clear. "I'll come back. Little Plum Blossom— or I

will send for you— I must go!" What was the matter
with his head? I must go— don't make it so hard
for me— don't make it so hard for me."

She clung to him, as she talked— what did she
want of the house— without him, her protector, the
house would be nothing— take her with him— take
her with him! She broke into hopeless sobs. If he *must*
go— couldn't he wait— just a little while. Let her
persuade him to take her too. She couldn't live any
longer without him— she wouldn't! She wasn't a
little girl— couldn't he see that— she *wasn't* a little
girl, and she tore open the kimono that had covered
her loveliness.

"I must go— *I must go!*" muttered the man, and he,
too, was swaying dizzily. . . . "I . . . . must . . . .
go. . . ."

"But you *must* understand— you *must* know— I
shall die if you leave me," and she wrapped her soft
body around him. His face was aflame, and he buried
it in the cooling fragrance of her hair. What was
the . . . . matter . . . . with him. . . . From a great
distance, he heard an exultant laugh . . . . and the
roar of a thousand waters rushed over him.

Haghi removed his ear-phones, and rolled a cigarette.

THE TREATY

Dr. Matsumoto trusted messenger of his country roused himself to a benumbed consciousness—— "I must go to Kitty— I must go. . . . . ."

He could not breathe— the very ceiling seemed crushing down upon him— his head ached, dully. . . . Kitty . . . . Kitty. . . . . .

His nerveless hand fell back from his throbbing head to the cushions on which he lay . . . . "Kitty. . . . . ."

There was no answer. . . . . .

He raised his head, fighting for clearness— fighting to see— to hear— to understand—. An agonizing shake of his head helped— the very pain of the motion was a stimulant— and his senses returned. His eyes searched the room, and halted with a horrid fascination on the valise. There it stood, untouched, save for the pocket in the lid, which, ripped from its fastenings, proclaimed— cried aloud its terrible message: The treaty was gone! "Kitty— Kitty," he cried in his agony. "Little Plum Blossom. . . . . ."

And, then, he stood at military attention— a traitor at a court-martial.

He saw but dimly, and yet with terrible clarity, the flag of his country— the millions of eyes of his countrymen turned to that flag— and then turning upon him in bitter reproach. Before him, as he gazed at the great tapestry that covered the hidden microphone, rose three blood-stained and distorted faces— those of the three men to whom he had but so short a while ago delivered the three envelopes, one of which was supposed to contain the treaty.

Had they spoken, or was it some greater voice— or an echo: "The man who does not deliver his envelope, with seals unbroken, to his Emperor, is not worthy to be called a Japanese!"

Dr. Matsumoto bowed his head. He had heard the verdict and accepted it without question. There was no further death for him . . . . ! "Kitty!"

With meticulous care he arranged his personal affairs— very calmly and deliberately. He wrote two letters one to the Japanese Minister, a terse, self-accusative message; the other he addressed to Number 326. After long consideration, he wrote another brief note: "May your Master have paid you well for what you have abandoned!" This note he took with him.

As the cool fingers of the dawn caressed the sleeping city, Dr. Matsumoto opened the door of the room in which he was about to return his soul to his ancestors. With the closing of the door, he shut out all of the Western world, save that small note addressed

He heard the verdict and accepted it without a question.

to Kitty, for this was a piece of the East— age-old and unchanged.

In one corner stood a black and gold lacquer chest, and from it, Dr. Matsumoto slowly lifted his black and white shroud— his death-robes, that were embroidered with his family crest and coat-of-arms. With even deeper reverence, he raised from its resting-place his dagger, with its twelve-inch blade— encased in its marvellously carved ivory sheath.

The walls of the room were of bamboo and rice-paper; straw mats alone covered the floor— mats bound in black. An ancient shrine stood in one corner— before it the pillow on which he was about to die. He opened the shrine. He placed the three incense burners so that their fragrance might rise in a column to his gods, and lighted them.

He dropped upon his knees on the cushion, and crossed his feet. He laid the dagger before him, and bowed in reverence to the shrine and to the future he sought. He lifted his palms, and softly rubbed them together in the ordained manner. His lips formed the old words of supplication: *"Namu Amida Butsu."*

Slowly he unfastened his black robe, and let it slip from his shoulders, loosened the girdle that bound in his waist, and opened wide his silk shirt. He tenderly removed the sacred dagger from its sheath, and, holding it between his thumbs, laid it back on the floor again. Then he encased the gleaming blue steel in a covering of rice-paper, and grasping it firmly in his hands, plunged it deep into his belly.

It was his own left hand that had driven the sacred dagger to his death, but it was the hand of the traditions of countless generations which had pressed it unflinchingly to its mark, and had held it firmly to its fatal course.

The hand of the dying man withdrew the blade of the sacred knife, removed the protecting film of rice-paper from the unblemished steel, and returned the blade to its sheath. His final duty was done. His body swayed from side to side for a moment in a silent agony, he clutched in his hand the brief note to that "innocent child" who had betrayed him to his shame—and his body sinking forward, the soul of Dr. Matsumoto passed to his ancestors. The blue smoke from the incense tapers rose pungently to the senseless nostrils of his gods: *"Namu Amida Butsu."*

CHAPTER XV

ON the great desk before Haghi lay three envelopes. They were all exactly alike, even to the strings that tied them and the seals that held the strings, except that, red as the seals themselves, untidy blotches stained the wrappings. Haghi looked at them with his expressionless eyes, and then picking them up slowly, without having opened them, dropped them one by one into the waste-basket beside him.

He pressed a button on the desk.

When Morrier entered, Haghi was rolling his inevitable cigarette. The assistant stood silently waiting.

Haghi finished his cigarette, carefully turning the paper at the end, placed it in his mouth, and leaned backward for the light that he knew Petra would hold ready for this movement.

"Morrier. In three and a half minutes Kitty will be here. She has the treaty with her. This is her re-

217

ward." He held up a magnificent string of pearls.
"When she has delivered the treaty to me, and has
sufficiently thanked me for these evidences of my
satisfaction, she will leave. You will follow. I shall
not care to see her again, Morrier— she is a bit too
cold-blooded, even for me, and she knows too much,
now. You understand?"

Then, as at the wave of his hand, the man started
to depart: "Just one thing more, Morrier— you will
bring the pearls back to me."

He lifted the telephone from its place: "Send Sonia
Nicholovena to me, as soon as Kitty has left."

Sonia entered the room as white as ivory; not
from the long confinement, but from the mental strain
under which she had been. Her skin was almost
transparent, as if blood no longer flowed beneath it.

"I have sent for you, Sonia, my dear," said Haghi
softly, "because I need you." She did not answer.

The sound of a closing door broke the silence.
Sonia looked about hastily— the room was empty,
except for Haghi and herself— the ever-present Petra
had disappeared.

"Yes, Sonia," continued the purring voice, "I need
you, and I have sent Petra away that I may tell you

how much." His smile seemed to lack its usual cynical assurance— it was almost sad. He held out his hand to her, but the girl remained on the far side of the table, motionless, with head erect, showing to him a face he had never seen before— a new face, transfigured with sorrow, pain, and determination, from which shone eyes made more luminous than ever by countless tears.

"So you will not touch my hand?"

"I will not, Haghi," she answered firmly.

"This man— this Number 326— you are quite sure of yourself— you love him?"

"I do!" replied Sonia, with a world of conviction in her voice.

"Then," said Haghi, "I have lost."

The girl made no comment.

For an interminable time the silence was unbroken. The man seemed to sink into his chair; his head dropped upon his breast.

"Sonia," he said at last, "I can see that this is the end. I had had hopes, my dear, hopes of which I have never given you even a suggestion. My visions were glorious to me— you and I working together for our great ideal, that was real— but beyond that sprang a hope— a desperate hope that at some time you might be blinded by the love within my eyes to the crippled body that holds me in its deformity.

"And now I know that my visions have faded— that I have lost you. This other man— a tool of those great evils that we were fighting together— has caught you, and stolen you from me, because he is straight in body and walks on two legs instead of moving on wheels. Yes— I know I have lost! And Sonia, you have been with me long enough to remember that I never play a losing game. I am withdrawing now— you are free— free to go where you will, and free from further interference from me or the Organization. The pledge of your oath of secrecy must alone remain sacred— everything else you may forget— even crippled Haghi. Perhaps, if we live, you may be glad to have known him."

The girl was aghast. There was timbre to his voice she could not believe could come from Haghi, the imperturbable —a ring of warmth and a pathos that was real. Could this man after all be human, did he suffer as had she at the things they each had done for the Cause? And his love for her. . . . . . ?

Then, through her bewilderment echoed the words: "you are free". . . . Free!— She swayed; her hands dropped to the table for support, and she felt the hand she had spurned close upon them.

"Does it trouble you so much as this— to be freed from me?" Where did the tenderness in his voice come from? "It has been so hard, Sonia, to hold to cold business— orders— brutal, necessary orders that have torn out my heart at times. To be stern to you, when my arms that are not crippled ached to hold you — I never realized before now how wonderful the touch of a woman's hand could be—"

He ceased abruptly; but as he placed her hand upon the table between them it was as if he had relinquished a most precious jewel.

"I am sorry, Sonia, that I have spoken as I did. These thoughts should have been kept for my own sorrow alone. They will never be mentioned again."

His head again dropped low upon his breast, and Sonia felt a strange pang of sympathy for this cripple — this idealist— this man who had so conquered his handicaps as to rule millions of men and of money.

When he raised his head again, Sonia looked into the eyes of the Haghi she had always known— and yet the past few moments gave her an insight not vouchsafed to her before.

"There is one matter of business," he snapped in

his old way, "before that matter of freedom. I told you I had sent for you because I needed you. I do. The greater need you have spurned— forgive me, Sonia— the lesser need is this: here is the treaty that means life or death to the interests of those who condemned to death your father and brother! I have never told you, because the time was not yet ripe, that I know— and know well— the man who pronounced upon them that infamous sentence. But now I tell you that it is vitally to his interest that the contents of this treaty do *not* reach the address to which you, as your last service to the Cause, are going to take it."

He gave her no chance to reply.

"Our enemies— and the police of the city here, instigated by them— have clamped down the most impenetrable barriers— even the faggot-bearers in the woods are being searched. . . . . ."

"What are you talking about," gasped Sonia. "What treaty. . . . . ?"

"You fool— oh! forgive me, my dear," the man caught himself. "Here, this treaty!"

He handed to her a tiny package; it looked like a small pack of solitaire cards: It was a collection of photographs— reduced prints of the papers that had brought clever, lovable little Kitty to her pearls— and her disappearance.

"It was unfortunate," said Haghi, "that such a gentleman as Dr. Matsumoto— a man of the highest intelligence— should have remained subject to an ancient, racial superstition. When he found that the treaty had been— abstracted . . . . he ran true to form— as they say on the race-tracks. . . . . ."

"You mean . . . . ?" asked Sonia.

"Yes," replied Haghi, sadly, "he committed hari-kari."

"And, Kitty?"

"Oh!" chuckled Haghi, "don't worry about Kitty. When I last saw her, she waved at me from the door there the great string of pearls that I had given her for her success in the advancement of the Cause. And, Sonia," he allowed himself an old-time cynical smile: "she bit each pearl in the whole string!"

It was the first time that Sonia had ever heard this man laugh, but as he finished his remark, his smile outgrew itself, until it broke into a chuckle and then into a full-grown laugh. His unusual mirth was interrupted by the ringing of his private telephone. "No!— No, I tell you, Morrier— bring them later!"

"And, now, Haghi, what is it you want me to do?"

223

Her voice was hard; her face was set like granite; her hands were clenched— free . . . . to be free from him. . . . "What is it you want me to do?"

"Deliver this here." He pushed aside the papers that had accumulated on his desk, "here." He handed her a memorandum. "This must be in Paris before ten o'clock to-morrow morning. There is no one but you, Sonia— it *must* be there— for the Cause— perhaps you could— er— persuade— your. . . . . . !"

"No," replied the girl, with a definite finality, "but, if it is possible, the delivery will be made."

Haghi smiled a wry smile. "Sonia, I am now learning the truth of that fatalistic remark of another idealist: 'as ye sow, so shall ye reap.' I have sown— with the exception . . . . no . . . . of that I have said I will not speak— and I— No! Sonia— not I— but our Cause will reap! And though I may seem to you— after what I have ill-advisedly said, Sonia, to be speaking of my own interests— think— think of the Cause! Bring this man of yours to the good work— if you can, Sonia— It is only for the Cause that I am speaking— myself . . . . I am nothing. That this man will ruthlessly destroy me, if he can find me— I *know!* He is blinded, as the rest of the world is blinded— by capitalism— the knout of to-day that

scourges the backs of the toilers— the producers—
and by its lashings gives by fear the power to those
that murdered your beloved ones— he is blinded, as
is the world. Sonia, my lost dear one, you can en-
lighten him— win him over to our side."

The woman had reached far within the files of
her memory— why? Haghi emotional . . . . ?
Haghi pleading. . . . . . ?

She reached also for the photographic reproductions
of the treaty, apparently ignoring the figures on a small
sheet that lay beside them. They were caught by her
trained memory: L/D/Z 10.16/33 133 Nr. 8.

She lifted the copy of the treaty— she took from
him the tickets and the passports which he had provided and offered to her, and accepted with the habit
of years the instructions that came to her.

"Then, this is good-bye, Haghi. I have been
honoured by what you have said to me— and I thank
you for my freedom from an oppression that made me
doubt you— and even the Cause! . . . . The treaty
will be delivered."

What were those figures on that paper? Why had
his hand moved toward it, and then withdrawn? . . . .
And then, lifting it, and folding it as calmly as he
would have rolled one of the papers of his inevitable

cigarettes, dropped it to one side— but folded, so that she could no longer read the numbers! No longer read them? . . . . did any written thing escape her skilled eyes: L/D/Z 10.16/33 133 Nr. 8.

She repeated his directions with the utmost precision, she again bowed to him with the distance of regal condescension, and left the room.

As the door closed behind her, Petra entered, and took up her silent stand behind Haghi's chair. The man could feel the eyes boring through his head. He turned in irritation.

"Well, what now?" he snapped. "Wasn't I convincing? Doesn't *she* still believe in the Cause?"

"Are you nothing but an actor— a cheat— a charlatan . . . . a devil?" Haghi interrupted her tears; his voice was that of a querulous child: "Must I fight you, as well as the rest of the world? You may go!"

CHAPTER XVI

NEMO-THE-CLOWN

NUMBER 326 was in an ill-temper when he reached his hotel on his return from his futile trip in pursuit of the dead Jellusic; completely futile unless the banknotes could be traced.

Franz met him with the word that a Japanese had been waiting for him for hours, refusing to give him, Franz, any message, also that Chief Jason had telephoned that he wanted to see Number 326 as soon as possible.

"Won't they even give a fellow a chance for a bath," growled the weary man.

He walked to the lobby of the hotel, fully expecting to see Dr. Matsumoto. Instead he found himself facing a stranger, a rather unobtrusive individual, who arose at his approach, and bowed. Number 326 looked at him questioningly.

"I was ordered to hand you this letter," said the

227

Japanese in a guarded tone. "I offer my apologies if I have seemed insistent, but my instructions were definite— that I hand it to you personally, and to you alone."

"I am sorry that you were kept waiting so long," replied Number 326. "I have just this moment returned to the city."

"Time is of no consideration when one has a duty to perform," said the Oriental.

Number 326 reached out his hand for the heavy letter.

"You have come from Dr. Matsumoto, I suppose," he asked.

"No," replied the man after a barely noticeable hesitation. He bowed deeply, and was gone.

Number 326 broke the seals of the envelope and tore it open. It contained some clippings, some pictures, and a letter. He saw the beginning words, and stared at them aghast, then, throwing himself into the nearest chair read:

"MY DEAR FRIEND:

The man who took the liberty of giving another man unasked for but still good advice has had occasion to need such advice for himself, and in learning his need of it has met his death. Do not waste sympathy on me, I

228

am unworthy of it. Also death is a portal through which we all must pass and it is none the harder to do so because one must open the door for oneself.

I am sending by a trusted messenger what I am no longer able to deliver to you personally; a clue that will lead you to the woman, who in turn will prove a clue that will lead you to the man for whom you are hunting.

And when you finally get him, Number 326, crush the life from this arch-fiend, not because he is a murderer, not because he is a double traitor who traffics in national honour for personal gain, but because he considers sympathy a crime and turns charity into a criminal offence. He strikes against the very foundations on which man's faith is built. To attain his own ends he ruthlessly breaks those eternal laws of kindness that are the music of the universe, breaking men's spirits and crushing their souls.

This is the crime for which your Christian Bible says there is no forgiveness . . . . the crime against the Holy Spirit.

Now, I must go, having failed. You will remain and will succeed. I must die, but you will live to accomplish your purpose. At the very portals of Death where I stand, I salute you as I turn to enter the Unknown.

MATSUMOTO."

The letter dropped from the hand of Number 326, as he stared into space. First, Jellusic . . . . and now, Matsumoto— two men of whom he had known nothing until he had undertaken this search and both dead within forty-eight hours of each other— who would be the next one? Himself? He shrugged his shoulders; life seemed to him at the moment of little value.

"A clue to the woman . . . ." the words seemed to call from the letter on the floor. He picked up the clippings and the pictures that Dr. Matsumoto had enclosed. They were from old Russian newspapers. A blurred print of a trial— Pictures of . . . . his heart leaped . . . . Baranikowa. . . . . .

He read the clippings— He ran through the pictures rapidly, and seized upon a small one that had evidently been an insert— the daughter— A young girl, and even the distortion of the newspaper photograph had not been able to destroy the loveliness of the face that looked at him . . . . Sonia . . . . Sonia. . . . It was the face he knew and the difference of the years was as nothing. "Oh! God!" he cried, "that you can be such a poisonous thing." A moment later he tore the picture from his lips, and flung it with a gesture of horror upon the floor.

He was aroused by a touch upon his shoulder. Franz stood beside him. "Well— what is it?" snapped Number 326, in unreasonable irritation.

"Mr. Jason is on the 'phone, sir."

NEMO-THE-CLOWN

Miles Jason was not awaiting Number 326 in his office, but in the theatre dressing-room of a man whose professional face was familiar to everybody— a face that had grinned and grimaced from a thousand billboards for weeks. "Nemo-the-Clown," the posters announced— and nothing more; it was sufficient.

The man had proved a strange genius— a clown and yet more than just a clown— an unexplainable delight. His act had been an inexplicable success. A mixture of slap-stick— of real musicianship on a freak instrument— of caustic and absurd comment, he caught his audiences in an instant by a personality that leaped across the footlights. That intelligent people would come again and again to see this grotesque figure, wearing shoes only a little smaller than an ironing board, made up to a typical clown's face, with enormous eyes and a huge mouth, potter about the stage, colliding ridiculously with everything, and shooting everything in mock exasperation with a toy pistol, was unbelievable. And yet so perfect was the man's artistry in his absurd rôle that when, having vanquished his annoying enemies, he would sit down happily upon his hands and joyously applaud himself with his enormous feet, the audience, night after night, rocked with uncontrollable laughter. Nemo had become an institution.

Miles Jason, in his dinner-coat and a bad temper, felt out of place among the confusion of grease-pots, jars of cosmetics, and the paraphernalia of the make-up table and dressing-room.

"Sit down," he growled, as Number 326 entered— a word to the door-man had passed him immediately.

"Now, listen, with both ears, because I've no time to repeat things twice. 326, this is Number 719. He has some valuable information for you. That's why I sent for you to come here."

The clown reached out his hand to Number 326, acknowledging the introduction, and Number 326 felt a sudden attraction and respect for this man whose keen eyes twinkled through his absurd make-up— a man who had achieved such over-whelming success in the profession he had adopted apparently merely to conceal his activities in the work of the Secret Service. Number 326 grasped the extended hand with a grip of cordiality— he was amazed at the physical power that answered him.

"An international treaty," the Chief was continuing, "has been stolen within a few hours of its signing. The man entrusted with the delivery of the copy stolen

232

is dead— by his own hand— your Oriental friend, Dr. Matsumoto, 326. Three men that were known to have left him within ten minutes after the signing of the treaty have been found dead— murdered. The woman whom your friend the Jap found wet and weeping in a door-way the night after he left you his good advice, 326, cannot be found. Some of the clothes she was wearing when last seen have been. There is only one answer— it is the work of this man we *must* get. Now, go ahead 719."

"I have not time," began the clown, quickly, "to go into the details of how I secured my information." The tone of his voice was in strange contrast to the ridiculous face from which it issued. "Your wire about the bank-notes mailed by Jellusic to himself was my starting point— I ran them down— their issuance was only a clue, I won't take time to tell you about them now— but following this clue led me to the plan to steal the treaty, and to the certain knowledge that there will be an attempt to send a copy of it to-night, despite all the precautions that the Chief, here, has taken to establish an unbreakable cordon about the city, to the very hands it must not reach, unless the world is to be plunged again into war, and a war that will destroy the governments of the world." The man's certainty was convincing beyond any doubt— he knew!

"To keep my value to the Service, 326, I cannot go. The Chief agrees with me that you are the one. I have found that the messenger will go by one of two trains, the through express or the one that leaves a short time before, and stops to pick up passengers from intermediate stations, and which the express overtakes. It seems to me that the logical thing for the messenger to do would be to take not the express but the first train. There would be less chance, he would think, of a close examination on this train. The Chief agrees with me, and we have reserved a ticket for you on it. Here it is—L/D/Z/33 133 Nr. 8.

"I speak of 'he,' the messenger. It may not be. There is a certainty, however, that it will be one of two people — a renegade who has been known by the name of Morrier, a man of medium height with a small black moustache, and an ever-present smile. If it is he, shoot him like a dog, for he is one. The other maybe a woman— more treacherous even than the man— Sonia Baranikowa— the vicious and vengeful daughter of an executed Russian revolutionary— a woman whose whole idea in life is the overthrow of government."

Number 326 staggered. The Chief, his head sunk upon his chest, did not notice, but the clown sprang from the chair before his mirror, and caught him. "Forgive me, 326— I had forgotten. My investigations brought me a knowledge of your— your personal — misfortune. I should have remembered— forgive me."

"But," he continued, and a ring of steel-hard authority was in his voice, "if you find this woman, 326, you must put aside your personal feelings— she must be destroyed!"

Chief Jason had lifted his head, and was eyeing the two men closely— the ridiculous clown, who spoke as a leader, a master— the exquisitely groomed young man whose face was that of a dead man. "He is right, boy."

Number 326 stood erect. "What time does the train leave?" he asked. "Good, I can make it comfortably. Thank you, 719, you may have solved more problems than you know."

With a salute to the Chief of the Secret Service— a suddenly old man, who looked after him with sad eyes — he left the room.

Ten minutes later, the audience was roaring with uncontrollable mirth at the antics of Nemo.

CHAPTER XVII

33 133

"THE gentleman in 119-120 was here for less than an hour at noon to-day, Madame, but he is gone," said the clerk at the desk of the Olympic.

"You have no idea where he went?"

"No, Madame, he left no word."

"Thanks," said the girl dully, turning away. The hotel lobby was crowded, and she threaded her way slowly through the mass of people, hoping against hope to see the beloved face she so longed to find. She wandered through the writing and the reception rooms — if he had returned at midday, perhaps— there was always a chance— something might be bringing him back again.

She must find him— must see him, if only for a moment. . . . She was supposed to be on the train, but she was risking missing it in her irresistible desire of trying once more to find him and to explain. And now, he was gone . . . . and no one knew where . . . . nor for how long.

Tears welled to her eyes; she forced them back, she must not lose self control. A Spy— on the last detail — but a Spy nevertheless; and a Spy must never make herself conspicuous, not even by eyes reddened with weeping. . . . Haghi's best Spy— but for the last time. . . . . .

Nothing remained now, but to go on her distasteful errand and carry out her horrid, final promise to the best of her ability.

She left the hotel, and went directly to the station. Her train was ready, and she went to her compartment.

The train was not crowded. She entered the stuffy little section with a strange feeling of gratitude— it meant a few blessed hours of undisturbed solitude for her. She took off her hat and jacket. She unpacked her little white pillow which had been such a comfort on so many trains, and ships, and, having bathed her eyes— the eyes that still burned with unshed tears— stepped to the window to lower the shades.

Another train, evidently a long distance one for it was made up of sleepers, slid in upon the adjoining track. A man entered the compartment that halted exactly opposite to hers, the light in his section falling full on his face as he threw his hat on the berth.

The man was Number 326.

Terrified, Sonia shrank behind the folds of the coat which she had hung by her window. She must not . . . . she must not call to him . . . . she must not let him see her now. . . . Not until she had completed this last service— this service that bore the reward of freedom— could she even recognize the fact that this man existed, except as an enemy— the man above all to be avoided!

And yet it was all she could do not to stretch out her arms to him— to cry aloud the love that burned within her. How his face had changed. It had hardened— his mouth had grown grim and bitter— it was her fault. The girl's trembling fingers ached to smooth out the furrows that lined his forehead— her heart cried out with longing to be able to tell him the truth— the whole truth— and to have his eyes again look into hers as they had— oh! so long ago.

The man pulled down his shades. Sonia pressed her face closely to her window— too late. The other train was in motion. As it pulled out, the numbers on the car opposite to her blazed into her eyes: Number: "33 133!"

238

Sonia pressed her fingers up against her eyes. Where had she seen that number before? "33 133!" Where had she seen it? Where had she seen it? . . . . "33 133." There was an irritating swing to it, a fiendish rhythm. The wheels of the train caught it, "33 133 . . . . 33 133". . . . the clothes and the curtains in her compartment swayed to it . . . . "33 133 . . . . 33 133." She laid down without undressing, and shut her eyes to try and blot out those numbers; but they still glowed against her eyelids "33 133."

Number 326 was lying in section 8, in the sleeper marked 33 133. He had removed his coat and had stretched out on the bed with his hands behind his head. He was painfully wide awake. He had been reading the papers bequeathed to him by Dr. Matsumoto, and was further than ever from understanding them. That this woman for whom his whole soul cried had suffered— had suffered terribly— was only too evident, unless. . . . . .

In the papers he found further pictures of the trial of Sonia's father and brother. Even this newspaper reproduction, snapped by a reporter in doubtful lighting, showed clearly the faces of the condemned men and that of the man who was pronouncing sentence. A cold hard face, and yet one that might have belonged to

many men except for the eyes. He did not recognize
it, but the unusual eyes recalled to him someone he
could not quite place in his own mind. He studied the
condemned men . . . . *her,* father and brother. . . .
Could he never forget that woman?

Number 326 replaced the bequest of Dr. Matsumoto
in his pocket. As he slipped in the papers his hand
struck something hard. He pulled it forth. It was
the medallion that Sonia had pressed upon him at
Danielli's. As his hand automatically raised it to his
lips he uttered a sneering laugh. Had the window
been open the man would have hurled it out into the
night. The window was shut, and he hesitated and
replaced it in the pocket of his coat.

Number 326, when he had entered the train had instinctively noted his fellow travellers. Despite the
fact that, from what Number 719 had said, he was
almost sure that Sonia— his Sonia— was the
messenger, there was always the possibility of the man
719 had described.

Number 326 recalled that a man answering the pre-
dicted description had passed him on the station platform. The face of the man had not been that of a
Russian, but he was of medium height, he wore a small
black moustache, and Number 326 remembered dis-

tinctly the pleasant smile with which he had handed his bag to the porter. Number 326 almost subconsciously, had recorded in his mind the number of the section which this pleasant-faced traveller gave to the porter . . . . it was the one adjoining his own. Well — he might as well investigate now as later.

He walked into the corridor. The door of the adjoining apartment was open. The suspected man lay slumbering comfortably, despite the noise of the train, and the intermittent banging of his compartment door. Number 326 shook his head with a heart breaking conviction: then it *must* be Sonia.

Number 326 returned to his compartment, and, removing his coat and tossing it carelessly into the rack above his berth, loosened his collar and stretched himself wearily upon the unturned down blankets.

Through the black night, rushed the train. The engineer was busy, watching for the signals upon which his life and those lives in the many cars behind him depended; the conductor was busy sleeping; the porters were also busy, drinking. The passengers were emulating the conductor; all except the neighbour to Number 326. No one saw him leave his compartment and move stealthily to the forward end of Car No. 33 133, hesitate for only a short few moments at the forward platform, and leap to the car ahead.

Number 326 tossed in his weariness and his heartache . . . . Sonia. . . . . . !

The train roared on, the passengers slept, and the porters drank.

Number 326 woke with a start— something had slapped him in the face. As he rose, startled, the something slipped to the floor. It was the ivory medallion that Sonia Nicholevena Baranikowa, Super-Spy, had forced upon him with her assurances of the good luck that attended its wearer. He picked it up— the second time to-night that it had come to him— bringing bitter memories. Everything seemed to be slowing as he looked, his heart beats, his mind, even his ears for the click of the wheels on the rails were slowing— slowing— slowing. . . . ! He suddenly came to his senses. The car had stopped. There wasn't a sound.

Number 326 leaped to his feet and rushed to the window. There was absolute blackness outside. He sprang to the door, and tearing it open peered through the window of the corridor— blackness— silence.

For a moment he hesitated. He knew only too well the danger of a panic. That there was something wrong— horribly wrong— was more than evident. He must keep silent. He ran to the back of the car, the platform from which he could get a view on three sides. To the rear, in the dim distance, was a faint glob of light, to the right and to the left— utter blackness. The train was in a tunnel— and stopped.

Number 326 tore forward through the corridor of the motionless car to the forward platform. The broken connection between that car and the one that should have drawn it forward on its way were only too great an evidence of the deliberate wrecking that had been done.

From the front platform he could see the verification of the fact that car Number 33 133 was abandoned in a tunnel. He ran back to the door through which he had seen the man with the small black mustache. The compartment was empty. He pushed open the door a bit— he entered. The compartment was unoccupied and the covers of the bed had not been touched. There was no luggage in sight— nothing save on the ledge by the window a dispatch case. Number 326 seized this. The snap yielded unresistingly to the pressure of his thumb . . . . the case was not locked— it contained nothing but old newspapers.

A steaming fog was growing denser with every passing second, and Number 326 found it increasingly

hard to breathe the choking coal gas fumes that swept
into the car. He rapped sharply on the door of the
service room . . . . he received no response . . . . he
forced the door . . . . he found the room deserted.

. . . . .

Suddenly he heard a sound, far off in the distance
. . . . a faint rumbling . . . . louder . . . . and
louder it grew. The rails began to hum. He rushed
back through the stalled car, smashing at every door in
desperate endeavour to awaken the sleepers that awaited
the certain death rushing upon them.

Was he right. . . . ? He was at the rear of the
car . . . . Merciful God!!! A light blazed through
the darkness— the tunnel roared!

As the headlight of the following engine split
the blackness of the tunnel, Number 326, with an instinctive rush, reached nearly to the front end of car
No. 33 133.

The terrible roar of the collision deafened his ears;
he felt himself hurled forward— and a great blackness
enclosed him.

CHAPTER XVIII

THE WRECK

SONIA opened her eyes, saw the lights outside and felt the train slowing up. Of course, this was the frontier . . . . and yet that did not account for her sudden awakening— for this strange premonition. Fully aroused, however, she persuaded herself that she must have had a bad dream. A number seemed to float through her memory— a number . . . . what was it?

She went through the annoyance of the custom formalities, seemingly amazed at the extraordinary severity of them. An official demanded her passport. With a disarming smile Sonia handed it to him, and then with a righteous indignation resented the order to depart with a matron who would subject her to a personal examination.

Upon her return, the matron having with a quick nod assured the chief that she had found nothing, the latter apologized for the annoyance and handed to

Sonia her passport, behind the picture of which were the photographic copies of the treaty that he had unconsciously preserved so carefully for her.

She was about to re-enter the train but lingered with a deliberate, accustomed nonchalance at the door of the telegraph office. She always listened whenever she could. That was not only the natural woman of her but the trained operative.

A man burst through the doorway nearly knocking her off her feet. He did not stop to apologize, but, with an ashen face, shouted: "No. 71—dropped rear car 33 133— wrecked by No. 83!" The telegraph office was in uproar; questions were hurled in all directions— answered— telephone bells. Sonia had staggered against the door trying to recover her balance. The desperate exclamations within the room beyond her rang in her ears, and sounding like a tocsin came the numbers 33 133. As a man rushed from the doorway she grabbed him by the coat— No, he could not pass— not without telling her what had happened!

He tried to tear himself away, and gave up— he was in a grip that even his strength could not break.

"There has been a wreck," he shouted. "Damn you, let me go— End car No. 33 133 of train No. 71 decoupled in tunnel— Express ran into it head on. . . .

For God's sake, woman, let me go. . . . The relief
train is pulling out."

The ground beneath the girl's feet swayed— It
was not she that moved, that she knew . . . . her head
was terribly clear. . . . Now she knew where she
had first seen those numbers 33 133 . . . . Haghi's
desk— that paper he had folded . . . . "L/D/Z
10.16 33 133 No. 8". . . . . .

She thought no more. She went. . . . . .

To his dying day the engineer of the relief train
which rushed to the scene of the wreck remained uncertain whether it had been an apparition that he had
seen that night when, tearing along at nearly sixty miles
an hour, he saw a figure swing out of the blackness of
his coal car and the night and climb in to the cab of
his engine. A woman . . . . a demon . . . . the
spirit of will power in the shape of a woman. . . .
Every rule and regulation of the road was violated by
this woman, if she were a woman, and yet the veteran
engineer did not question her presence, but merely
opened his throttle wider. Perhaps because his fireman had made no remark, he questioned his own
senses.

For many years this master mechanic at the throttle
had driven through day and night the hurtling wheels

of his great locomotives, forcing at terrifying speed the whirl of those wheels that spun faster and faster under the merciless drive of money— money— money.

What a delight it was to know that now this race was one of mercy— great God it *was* a woman— he saw her clearly just as the airbrake screamed.

Through the pandemonium that reigned, through the flickering light of the torches, half smothered by the smoke curling from the mouth of the tunnel, men in dirtied uniforms that once were white were bearing on stretchers silent figures. These men coughed desperately— the acrid odors of burning wood and hot metal swept with the draft from the tunnel as a hellish accompaniment to the crackle of flames, the hissing of escaping steam, the clang of metal, the shrieks, the cries and groans, the vicious roar of the acetylene torches . . . . agony . . . . crushed mangled humanity . . . . commands . . . . names called over and over again, shrieked. . . . . .

As the engine stopped, Sonia had leaped from it. With the desperation, and the blindness of an unutterable devotion, this gentlewoman— gentle despite her terrible Service— forced her way past the human and mechanical wreckage that faced her.

Screams of agony turned the tunnel into an inferno.

THE WRECK

The huge locomotive like a great rampant beast had plunged on into the obstacle in its path. It seemed as if it had tried furiously to toss the obstacle out of its way, and, unsuccessful, had rammed its monster body through the centre of its foe, crushing and splintering it into fragments, and had come to rest a-top of its victim, and now hung panting and blazing away in a half-spent wrath.

A heap of embers at one side was spitting foul gases where the waters from the shattered boilers hissed on it— spitting drops that fell upon the unclosed eyes of the dead that were stretched in their silent row.

Sonia Baranikowa— Sonia, the Super-Spy— the woman who had been responsible, cold-bloodedly responsible, for the deaths of many men— died at that tunnel mouth. A frantic girl rushed into the blackness, stumbling through the smoke, choking on its bitterness. She came to where the feeble lights showed the faces of the remaining bodies— she had fought with the stretcher bearers for the sight of the faces of those that they bore.

No . . . . No . . . . No . . . . Thank God. She rushed on further into the blackness, the blackness that now was glowing with the fire of the wreck and the emergency lights of the relief crew. It was in the bril-

liance of the latter that she saw sitting on a shattered car seat, a woman, rocking from side to side— nursing a dead baby. She was singing a lullaby— singing it with horrible repetition. Oh God, the other horrors
. . . . .

At last, the car . . . . crushed like an egg shell. . . . All but the side that gleamed in the light of the emergency torch— the side which bore the numbers 33 133. Upholstery, blankets, pillows, luggage and clothing exploded to every direction . . . . splintered, shattered glass . . . . twisted metal.

The girl stopped, no, she didn't stop. Fear had held her. Fear of what she might find— the man she loved— the man more to her than even her final pledge to Haghi . . . . the pledge from which she was now absolved by Haghi's own treachery. She forced her way through the wreckage and down the bent aisle.

Wreckage. . . . . .

From the floor of that twisted corridor, showing through the torn carpet, came a gleam of white. In a moment the frantic girl had torn aside the remains of that carpet. With a great gasp, she seized from the stiff fingers that held it, the ivory medallion whose white gleam had caught her eye.

252

THE WRECK

Like a mad woman, she crashed in the glass of the emergency tool-kit, and tore from it the crow-bar. She pried desperately— the arm came free— she could see his head— it moved . . . . ! Oh! God be thanked — he was still alive. But she could not free him from the great weight that held down his body. She cried — she shrieked for help. At the far end of the wreckage, she could see the glow of flames. She re-doubled her efforts— uselessly.

A hand dropped upon her shoulder— a voice sounded in her ears:

"And, so, my dear Sonia— this is the way you deliver your message?"

It was Morrier.

Her one thought was that here was help. "Oh! God bless you, Morrier— here lift this— pull— *pull,* man, and we can get him out before the fire reaches here!"

Then she saw the sneer on his face and the intent in his eyes. Wildly she swung her crow-bar, but the wreckage above her blocked its sweep. Morrier gripped her by the arms, and the strength of this slight man was astounding. She *knew* now.

"You devil," she shrieked— "it *was* planned then by that fiend Haghi— another *accident*——"

253

"Yes, my dear," Morrier replied suavely, restraining her struggles with ease. The terrific din of the rescue work— the crash of axes and sledges— the wild shouting of orders— the roar of oxy-acetylene torches whose flames were endeavouring to release the pinned down victims before the licking tongues of uncontrolled flame could grill the life from them— and all echoing, and re-echoing from the tunnel-walls— made him secure. He had plenty of time— the fire was still two compartments distant.

"Yes, my dear Sonia," he continued, "you are quite correct. It was planned— and you must admit very well planned. And, now, just what do you think ought to be done?"

The woman made no reply.

Morrier drew her two hands together, and slipped both wrists into the grip of one of his. She might as well have been handcuffed.

Very slowly, and with his ever-present smile, he reached backward with his free hand. With equal deliberation, the automatic pistol rose to her temple. She made no move. It was as if she were rigid with the terror of the death that must come to her in but a brief moment.

"The Chief, and the Organization, have decided that

your value to them has depreciated to an impossible degree, my dear Sonia. Therefore I shall relieve you of that copy of the treaty, which you have so cleverly concealed— that Customs Official was a fool, wasn't he? Nearly as great a one as our friend beneath us." He waved a slight aside to the limp hand that protruded from between the shattered planking— the hand of a dead man. "And, now, my dear, duty calls— and if I don't get out of here in a very few moments I won't get out at all. Er— I am commissioned to convey to you the great regrets of Chief Haghi that he is not able to be present to offer you in person his farewell compliments."

The pistol pressed closely against her forehead. What did it matter to her . . . .? Father . . . . brother . . . . and this unknown man who meant more to her than both. . . . She would find them waiting for her.

The trigger was not pulled— the blinding shock she had almost hoped for did not come. She felt the grip upon her wrists tighten and then relax. The pistol dropped slowly from nerveless fingers. It seemed to take an interminable time to reach the floor. Her eyes followed it, and saw the reason, for her release. About Morrier's ankle, the fingers of that "dead" hand had closed, and to him it must have been the hand of retribution, a hand whose grasp even the power of his beloved master could not loosen. She stared in unbelievable delight at the living tenseness of the hand. She raised her eyes to Morrier's face. It was ghastly. His eyes opened in a horrid fascination— his smile— Morrier's ever-present smile— was a set grin. His eyes opened wider— horror and fear leaped from them — and the woman saw a small hole appear, as if by magic, between those eyes.

Sonia paid no attention to the falling body of the dead man as it dropped. She clutched at the hand that held the pistol— it was limp in her grasp. She was crying aloud in her hysteria— "my Beloved— my Beloved!"

She managed to release his head, that slumped against her breast. She was wildly kissing him, and her tears dripped upon him. The flames were drawing closer. She strove desperately to free him— and hopelessly. Nearer and nearer crept the heat of the blazing wreckage. She folded his head close in her arms, and buried her face in his hair. The torture of the heat was becoming unbearable! She was strangling in the pungent, acrid smoke! A tongue of flame shot out and licked her hand. She withdrew it instinctively, and replaced it quickly as she realized that it alone had saved his face from the scorching inferno. There was but one thing she could move between him and the flames— the dead body of Morrier! With a strength at which she herself could but marvel she lifted the corpse— and hurled it into the mouth of the fire. She smelt the burning flesh . . . . her head sank. . . . . .

Devils were lifting her— devils, black-faced, and with horrible mouths— mouths twisted into caricatures of human mouths. . . . Devils— devils without human faces, only terrible, elephantine travesties of faces — horrible masks. . . . . .

CHAPTER XIX

REVELATIONS

IF that great bell would only stop . . . . if the terrible swaying would only cease— yes, yes— she knew it was her head that was ringing the bell— each blow struck like a sledge-hammer— she would let go, and not swing any more— and then her head wouldn't strike— and then the bell couldn't ring so— and then

. . . . .

Kisses upon her lips brought her back to consciousness. Her eyes opened in wondering unbelief— it was he— it was he—! What was he saying— she didn't care— his arms were about her— he was alive, and holding her close to him— that was all that mattered — his kisses— Beloved— beloved. . . . . .

What were they doing to her? They were hurting her hand. Why didn't he stop them— why didn't he stop them— why didn't he kiss her again. . . . What were they saying . . . . drink this . . . . she didn't

want to . . . . they were leaving her alone . . . .
where was he . . . . why wasn't he kissing her.
. . . . .

She sat up— dimly seeing. There were horrid cries
in the air— oh! if they would only stop— Where *was*
he—?

A white-coated figure was bending over a still form
prostrate beside her. In the faint light she could just
see— but, as at the sound of her movement the bending figure turned its head, she shrieked! Sonia
Nicholovena Baranikowa was no longer a woman—
she was a tigress. She sprang! The shock drove
the white-coated man sideways, and he fell, dropping the tiny syringe he had held in his hand.
The struggle for the possession of this rolled back
and forth over the body of Number 326, until it broke
the faint of relief into which his senses had dropped.
A man fighting a woman! Number 326 swayed dizzily to his knees, and swung a feeble blow at the brute.
He fell again with the exertion, and fell to break the
hold of the woman. The "doctor" leaped to his feet,
and tore off!

It was *her* kisses that woke him, now. "Beloved—
beloved—!"

A miracle— yes— but his head cleared!

". . . . he is one of— Us! He was going to poison you! Look— he has gone to warn the Chief!"

Number 326 staggered to his feet. He could see the running figure, throwing aside its white coat, rushing toward a car that was drawn up to the roadside. Behind it he thought he could see a motor-cycle — a police machine, perhaps, and if so faster than any car.

As he ran toward the road, the very effort burned the haze from the brain of Number 326. When he leaped upon the stolen motor-cycle, every nerve was vibrant with but one idea— get him— even Sonia was forgotten.

That chase— that ride at impossible speed— is still the talk of the tiny hamlets through which car and motor-cycle roared and spat. Number 326, to this day, remembers nothing of it. The crash wiped it all from his mind. He can recall only the passing of the car he was pursuing— a desperate resolve— his quick swing in front of the rushing machine— and then the sharp *tings* of the wire spokes of his motor-cycle wheels— like breaking banjo-strings— as the automobile passed over them.

It was ages later.

REVELATIONS

"Yes, damn it— I know— I know," he heard a harsh voice growl, "but he isn't a baby, even if he did land in .a baby-carriage. He isn't hurt— I know him! You can't hurt him! And you medicos are too damned fond of coddling people in bed— and keeping them there until they are really sick. He's just tired, that's all. That's what's the matter with him, and it won't hurt him in the least."

He knew this voice— he had certainly heard it before. Who was it that always roared in this way?

"Do you want to see me cure him? No, I won't stop! You just watch, and learn something— and don't anyone of you move, or I'll put you all under arrest. SONIA!" The great voice bellowed forth the word.

Number 326 started. His fully conscious eyes had but a moment to see the aghast faces of the shocked doctors and the orderlies about the bed on which he had been lying— his ears but a moment to hear the guffaw of relieved laughter that burst from the throat of Chief Jason— and then she came. He did not see the bandaged hand— the singed hair— the great bruise on her face. His whole soul poured into the deeps of those eyes that were so radiant before his

261

own, his senses became as nothing. . . . Sonia. . . . Sonia. . . . . .

"Leave him alone!" He heard that roaring voice again. "I tell you it's the best medicine in the world — and I never thought I'd hear myself say it."

The woman in his arms felt Number 326 stiffen. She was grasped by the shoulders— shaken to the actual, and the dream-moment vanished. She looked at him. Here was not the man she loved— here was Secret Service Operative #326— on duty!

His glance flashed about the room. In a heap upon the chair in the corner lay the clothes they had stripped from him. With no thought for the proprieties, and avoiding the restraining hand of the doctor, he leaped from his bed, and seized his coat. Into his pocket he plunged his hand, and snatched forth the clippings sent him by Dr. Matsumoto. Back to where the girl sat on his bed-side he sprang, and held one of the clippings before her. There was a power and certainty in his voice that made the doctor's eyes open in astonishment, and made him turn in gaping wonder to Chief Jason. And the latter, with hands thrust deep into his coat pockets, and with jaw thrust far forward, made no sign— but looked and listened.

It was cold, and strong, and certain— yes— this

voice of Number 326— a man who but a few instants ago had been a senseless clod; but, cold though it was, there was a warmth of triumph in it— strong and certain— yet a tremble of eagerness.

"When you spoke to that accomplice of yours— in the car— that member of your great organization— you used a name. That name was 'Haghi'— ! Answer me— is he your Master? Then look!"

She had closed her eyes, but the command in his tone forced them open. Before her she saw a picture of a courtroom— the jury to the right— the judges at the centre— and at the table of the men on trial for their lives her father and her brother. Their faces leaped from the cheap and faded newspaper half-tone. For one silent moment— a moment of prayer — she bowed her head; then, her eyes focussed on the face of the central judge in the picture that was held relentlessly where she must look. Number 326 had not shifted his eyes from her for an instant, and the fixed gaze of Chief Jason was as set as the undershot jaw. The doctor and the orderlies did not know where to look— something was happening that made them feel distressingly uncomfortable.

Sonia, like a person hypnotized, stared at the face in that old newspaper print, stared at the eyes, then a flame of hatred leaped from her lips: "HAGHI!" it screamed.

"No," said Number 326, carefully refolding the picture, and giving a quick glance at his Chief, "no— not Haghi, but Dimitri Michailovitch Ochgolski!"

CHAPTER XX

RUN TO EARTH

HAGHI, the imperturbable— the cold-eyed— tore the receivers from his ears, and slammed them upon the great desk. The flood of reports pouring from the chute at his right covered them, and through the muffling of the papers they spoke feebly— more and more so as the pile increased. He rolled a cigarette. He turned his head for Petra to light it, and for the first time in years noticed the trembling of the hand that held the match for him. He turned farther.

The woman stood, as usual, with a mask of a face, and yet the stony blankness of the eyes was missing— there was a light in them.

"What do you mean?" snapped Haghi— "what do you mean by looking at me that way?"

The graven immobility of the face into which he glared did not change, but the light in the eyes grew

SPIES

brighter. She made a slight motion of her hand toward the ear-phones, now completely buried.

"Well— and what?"

"Listen," she said. "It is the end. . . . . ."

"Listen to what?"

She pointed silently to the growing heap of papers.

The man wheeled his chair with a motion so vicious that the back struck his white-garbed attendant before she could move. "Listen to what?" He was like a cobra, ready to strike. "Speak, can't you— speak!"

"Is it any fault of mine that I do not speak? Who has made me keep a silence all these years? Shall I speak now at your bidding? You would better listen to what my ears can hear— those ears that you have made me use instead of the tongue that you have kept silent. Listen!"

She stepped forward quickly, whirling about the chair of the seated man as she did so, and swept from the discarded ear-phones the mass of unheeded reports that had muffled the words that now rang faintly from them:

". . . . and now they've got me . . . . look out for . . . . 326 . . . . I . . . ." The voice stopped.

"Did you hear what he said before?" snapped Haghi.

"I never hear anything that you do not hear."

266

RUN TO EARTH

The woman was again a figure of stone with eyes of jade.

Haghi became almost vibrant with motion. His fingers played in chords upon the buttons of the great desk. From telephone— from chute— from hidden speakers came reports. He listened— he read at a glance and destroyed— he listened—!

And then came orders. From the centre of his web this spider vibrated every thread of it. Close the shops that hid his stronghold— double-guard each entrance and exit— all within the building to arm and to wait further orders— no one to be admitted—

Why didn't Morrier come? Must he ring forever. He lifted the phone again. Then he remembered!

He swung about to Petra. "You must go. Here!" He wrote a pass for the woman, reached into the desk and pulled forth a handful of bank-notes: "Here. A passage on plane 473 that leaves at. . . . . ."

He stopped. The woman was not listening to him, her eyes were on the ear-phones, and she was bending toward them. He gripped the hand that reached forward, and seized the phones. Before her other hand had torn loose the wires he had heard the end of the report: ". . . . in his car will pass through No. 22 . . . reach No. 43 in ten minutes. . . . ."

SPIES

He crashed the useless instruments upon the head of the woman, who fell senseless to the floor.

"Franz," Number 326 had said, "Franz, I am leaving you in charge of the most precious thing in the world. You are now taking my place in guarding it. I don't have to tell you that I trust you, but I tell you that *you* must not trust even yourself! Drive through the back streets, and when you get to the hotel lock her and yourself in. Don't let anyone— even me— come in until you have first received this." He held out the ivory medallion.

Franz had been silent. Neither of his two remarks would have applied to the occasion. He had watched his master bend tenderly over the drooping figure in the back of the car— kiss passionately a hand that strove to hold him back— and tear himself away.

As the door slammed, Franz began to obey his orders. The car leaped forward. Through every back way that he knew, he threaded his path, toward that narrow alley-way that ran behind the hotel. There he could leave the car in charge of his friend the rear-porter, and smuggle his master's lady up to his rooms, without even the elevator men having seen her. There could not have been a better plan, had it not been

With an ear-splitting roar the cocoanuts exploded.

for that half heard telephone message to his chief from the "vagabond" who had heard the directions of Number 326, had ridden the spare tire far enough to know where Franz was headed, and had reported.

"Only a few moments more," the faithful Franz had thought as he turned into the narrow alley. He had been forced to slow more than he liked, and now it was even worse— the street, if it could be called a street, was cluttered and nearly blocked by the overturned pile of building material that had spilled across it. The one side of the street that was free was barred by the cart of a peddler— a vender of cocoanuts. He resented the appearance of the car— he resented the summons of the horn— he resented almost everything; that is, from his actions. He did not move his cart, but merely shrugged his shoulders; and with a scurrilous gesture indicated to Franz that the chauffeur and his car could take either the road over the building material or the path to Hell.

Franz had climbed from the automobile, and had moved forward to push back the cart. The peddler had been thrown into an unreasonable rage— he had seized two cocoanuts from his rickety vehicle, and had hurled them at the advancing chauffeur. There had been a shrill whistle— a terrific roar as the cocoanuts exploded— a strangling, as the whole air filled with the pungent fumes— a rush of men from the building whose unused material had spilled into the street— and Franz, fighting like a demon, felt himself lifted into the back of *his* car— knew that the car was moving— and that was all.

The children that were on the scene of the "explosion" within the neglible number of seconds necessary to bring them there— the gas, at that, had held them off for several— helped themselves freely to the cocoanuts that remained on the now unattended cart. They were good cocoanuts— exceptionally good ones, too, — not quite ripe, and full of milk.

CHAPTER XXI

THE TAKING OF THE BANK

ALMOST at the moment of the explosion of the "cocoanuts," Miles Jason, Chief of the Secret Service, and Number 326 were being received by one of the directors of Haghi's bank.

"What can I do for you gentlemen?" he asked politely, though his forehead was beaded with perspiration.

"We wish to see President Haghi," replied Jason.

"I am sorry, very sorry," apologized the director, with a shrug of his shoulders, "but President Haghi is not in the bank at the present moment."

"Then go find him, and tell him to get here as soon as possible."

The man gave Jason a look of scornful contempt, but neither the Chief nor his aide paid any attention to the scorn or the anger in his voice.

"Aside from the fact that President Haghi does not

273

take orders from me *or* from you, Chief Jason, I haven't the faintest idea where he can be reached."

"That is a lie," said Jason sternly, "and a poor one." The director stepped forward quickly, his fists clenched; and drew back as quickly before the pistol held steadily in the hand of Number 326.

"You can afford to insult a man with a gun to back you up. But it won't do you any good— I don't know where he is."

"You are his chief representative?"

"Yes."

"Then hand over your keys. I want the combinations of the safes and vaults as well. . . . . ."

The director started to laugh, but Miles Jason crashed his huge fist down on the desk before him. "This is no time to laugh, sir," he roared. "You'll soon sing another tune. And don't stick too close to your 'President Haghi' either, if you know what is good for you. You might be mistaken for him, and you would find that damned uncomfortable. Now, are you going to hand over those keys?"

"I am not," said the man sullenly, and reached for the telephone.

"The wires are cut," said Jason curtly. "Who do you want?"

"The police," snarled the director, "to put an end to this outrage."

"I can help you then," replied the Chief. "It happens that for the time being I am in charge of the police, and by my orders they have surrounded this building, and are now only waiting for my signal before taking charge of it."

"What do you mean?" exclaimed the bank official, endeavouring to cover up his evident perturbation with a cloak of indignant surprise. "What have the police to do with Haghi's Bank? What do they want here?"

"A criminal and his gang," remarked Number 326 dryly.

The director gulped, but stuck to his guns: "Are you men forgetting that there is a law in this country. Do you realize that you are forcing an entrance to private property without warrant or even excuse. Do you . . . . ."

"We'll have a little talk about the law later on," interrupted Jason. "After we've finished here, and if you find yourself free, and if you feel still inclined, no one will stop you from invoking all the laws on the statute books. But now, listen to this!" he roared. "Right now, *I* am the law, and the only one! For the last time, will you hand over those keys?"

"I will not," replied the man doggedly. "I do not recognize your right. . . . . ."

The Chief nodded quickly to his aide, and Number 326, leaping to the window, threw it open. The shrill call of his police-whistle galvanized into action the battalion of uniformed police and plain-clothes men awaiting this signal. From every side they poured, storming the dignified portals of the imposing structure. It was but a moment's work to batter in the doors, through which they streamed, and spread to every part of the bank.

Orders were not necessary, these had been all given previously and in detail. At each safe, and at every vault door a crew worked feverishly with blow torches, preparing the way for the nitroglycerine to tear the doors apart. Others charged the cages, and rounded up the startled employees. Huge trucks rolled to the entrance of the bank, and into these were piled load after load of seized papers.

Leaving the Chief in charge of this work, Number 326, with a squad of picked men, searched inch by inch along the walls of an upstairs corridor for the secret door that led to Haghi's great hidden building. Sonia had told him that this door must be somewhere there, although she had never seen it herself. Tapping with hammers, drilling here and there, they made their way slowly— and without success.

A touch on his arm interrupted Number 326. He turned sharply from his intensive search to find a policeman at his elbow, saluting. The man held forth a note.

"What's this?" snapped Number 326.

"I was told to hand you this letter," replied the officer.

"By whom— where— when?"

"I don't know the man, sir. He gave it to me in the counting room two minutes ago."

"If you didn't know him, why didn't you hold him?"

"He said he was one of Chief Jason's men, sir."

Number 326 tore open the note and glanced at it. The written words struck from the paper like so many blows. He swayed on his feet, and leaned against the wall for support. A policeman coming to him for further orders stepped back in amazement; he looked inquiringly at the man who had delivered the letter, but the latter could only shake his head in equal perplexity. Hurrying footsteps came down the corridor. It was Miles Jason, to see how the search was progressing. The sight of Number 326's face brought him up short: "Good God! lad, what's the matter?"

Number 326 slowly raised his head. Even last night, with the locomotive rushing down upon him in the tunnel he had not looked like this. He tried to speak, but the words would not come. His mouth remained open— half-paralyzed. The Chief took the letter from his limp hand, and read:

"Unless this building is vacated within 15 minutes after the receipt of this message and the police recalled, the woman you love as well as the man you left in charge of her will both die. I have them at my mercy.

HAGHI."

"The damned devil!" exploded Miles Jason. He fixed his eyes firmly on Number 326, and his jaws closed with a snap. Number 326 raised a trembling hand, and wiped his clammy forehead. His Chief cleared his throat harshly. He was sick at heart. "Brace up lad," he said at last, "buck up! Now, we've *got* to find that door— that's our only chance— for we do not withdraw our men!"

Number 326 snapped to a salute: "Of course not, sir," he agreed, choking down a great sob. Then, turning, he shouted at the top of his lungs: "Men, we've got exactly ten minutes to locate and open that secret passage. The lives of two people depend on it.

278

The lives of a woman and a man are the stakes we are fighting for."

Miles Jason removed his shabby hat from his head. He was anything but a pious man, but he breathed with a deep sincerity his short prayer, "Oh, God, help the boy."

CHAPTER XXII

"I HAVE given your beloved one a last chance," Haghi was saying. "The last one for you and for him. . . . I don't quite understand it myself, but there is something about him that makes me want to be magnanimous. I rather admire him I think."

His old smile played about his lips, self-satisfied and mocking.

Sonia made no reply.

She was strapped to a chair, arms and body and feet, and, with eyes burning like coals in her white face, sat staring silently at the man behind the great desk. It was not hatred that shone from her eyes— it was not loathing, and still less terror. Her eyes were the eyes of the Angel of Death, and in them gleamed: "You are going to die, Haghi!" her eyes said: "You are courting and facing Death; not because you are a murderer and a thief— a firebrand; not because of your innumerable sins and crimes, but because you have betrayed and abused the faith of a friend."

"He is probably reading my letter now," continued Haghi suavely, "my note in which I informed him that you two are my prisoners— you and our gallant fighting Franz here. I've given him fifteen minutes to clear out and put the bank in order. Let's hope he will do so, Sonia; you are rather too beautiful to die."

The girl with the eyes of the Angel of Death did not reply, nor did she flinch.

Haghi toyed with the clock on his desk. "I'm beginning to think you do not consider it worth your while to answer me, Sonia."

"She's right," broke in Franz. He was tied and strapped to the back and legs of Sonia's chair; his eyes blackened and half closed, his face battered and bruised. It had taken the combined efforts of four men to subdue him, and two of these had been sent to the hospital as a result. "But if Miss Sonia wasn't in the room," he continued, "I'd answer you, you skunk, I'm just waiting for the chance."

"Well, my dear Franz," replied Haghi dryly, putting a mark on the clock dial, "you will have a long wait, and not much of a chance. When the minute hand of this clock touches that dot, I shall release poison gas throughout the entire bank. That will clear it out fast enough, I venture to believe. A minute after that, this door will open itself. That will be the moment of your death. Will you continue to keep silent, Sonia?"

There was no answer— only the steady eyes.

Haghi grew unnaturally pale. When he spoke again there was a new note in his voice; it seemed that he almost pleaded.

"If I give you the chance to write to him, would you ask him to go, to abandon his futile attempt to defeat Haghi, in order to save your life."

Sonia smiled.

"So you are *afraid* of him! You know that your end has come. Haghi is afraid!" She broke into a rippling laugh. "Yes," she continued, "if I had the chance I would write to him. Do you want to know what," she asked, her eyes shining. She leaned forward and spoke softly. "I'd write: 'Beloved, the woman you love is dead. She did not want you to save her life at the expense of your honour and duty. Therefore, she has died to leave you free to find and punish the devil you seek!' "

She rose in her chair as far as the straps would let her, and a terrible hatred rang in her voice: *"That* is what I would write to him— Dimitri Michailovitch Ochgolski!"

The man started in surprise, then, as he rolled a cigarette, his face set again in its usual impassiveness.

"So," he said at last, "you have recognized the old friend of the family. It is a pity, my dear Sonia, that the acquaintance on this new basis cannot last very long. You will notice from the clock that it is time for me to take my departure, just before you take yours. By the way, if you should happen to meet them, kindly remember me to your dear father and brother.

"Now, spend your last few moments in thinking how I have tricked you. You have learned more about me than I supposed, but not all. Here is your opportunity. . . . . ."

He pushed back the chair as he spoke, *rose gracefully to his feet,* and bowed ceremoniously. Sonia fell back with a gasp.

"And, now," he continued, as he slid aside the plate protecting the fatal button on his desk, "farewell, and— er— a pleasant journey."

With the last word his finger pressed down and held for a second. Then, straightening up, he walked past Sonia and Franz as if they did not exist. The door closed behind him, and the safety locks snapped.

The clock on the desk monotonously clicked off the seconds.

Sonia had ceased to struggle against her bonds, not from exhaustion, nor pain, but because of the hopeless futility. What chance had she ever had of besting this man— one clever enough to dupe her and many others, despite an almost daily contact with him, into believing that he was an invalid— a cripple— a helpless paralytic?

She stared in fascination at the tiny mark on the dial of the clock. The minute hand was drawing nearer and nearer. Silently, she steeled herself to accept her fate, but the tears rolled down her face as her thoughts turned to the love and the lover she must leave.

The exasperated shouts of Franz brought her to herself with a start. No longer the polite servant, he was cursing her roundly: "Damn you, woman! Can't you do something besides sitting there snivelling? Get to work with your teeth at these straps! Bite them through. I'm not ready to die before my time just because you're willing to sit there and do nothing."

The rough tone was like a dash of cold water in her face. Her teeth sank viciously into the straps that bound him. She worked desperately, forgetting even

The door swung suddenly open on silent hinges. . . . A shadow fell across the wall.

to look at the relentless finger of time on the face of the ticking clock. She forgot to listen for the opening of the door. Would that strap never give way? Bite— bite— bite! It *was* giving— she could feel it stretch under the strain of Franz's pull. Bite— bite! And then, the broken end was torn from between her teeth as with a great tug Franz snapped it. With his free hand, the man worked frantically. One leg— the other — was freed. Only one hand to clear. . . . . .

The door swung suddenly upon its silent hinges, admitting a shaft of light. A shadow fell across the wall. Sonia shrieked in warning, and Franz, with one final effort bursting the last bonds that held him, flung himself flat to the floor as the guard fired. The bullet sped over his prostrate body, and crashed through the clock dial. Instantly Franz sprang to his feet, snatched up what remained of the heavy metal time-piece, and hurled it with terrific force into the face of the man in the doorway.

He had aimed well. With a gurgling scream, the man clutched at his face and collapsed. But a second guard was already plunging over the body of the first. Franz threw himself upon him before he had time to catch his balance. The shock of the attack was so great that the deadly automatic in the hand of Haghi's man was knocked to the floor. It fell almost within the reach of the two, as they rolled over and over each other in their desperate struggle. The guard fought with the ferocity of an angry bull, but Franz, wild with fear for the safety of the woman he had told his beloved master he would protect at all costs, battled with the superhuman strength of a madman. Over and over they rolled, pounding, throttling, biting, till with a sudden supreme effort the guard's hand seized the pistol. A wild scream from Sonia— the roar of a shot! But Franz had struck with the quickness of a cat, and the bullet crashed upward into the ceiling!

On the other side of the wall, Number 326 and his men hammered frantically, and hopelessly, all except one. He was an insignificant little fellow, nicknamed Mousey, because of his habit of sticking his pointed nose into everything. He had stuck it into the office of President Haghi, and was measuring and tapping the walls of the small adjoining wash-room, when the muffled sound of a shot came to his ears. It must have been fired in the next building— the building whose entrance they sought! He raced about like a ferret, putting his ears against the tiles, tapping, shouting, and

288

then tore out of the door to find Number 326. The corridor was empty!

As he rushed for the stairway, a sudden paroxysm of coughing seized him. He could hardly breathe. He fought his way down the steps through a yellow fog that eddied and swirled. Men were staggering about, choking and strangling, struggling wildly to get out into the street. He saw Number 326 pleading with his men to go back, his face distorted with anguish as one by one they broke from his grasp and stumbled to the doorway.

Mousey seized him by the arm and tried to draw him toward the stairway, pointing upward. Number 326 stared blankly at him for a moment, and then, with sudden comprehension, leaped for the steps, with Mousey at his heels.

The corridor . . . . the office . . . . the wash-room . . . . a blank wall at which Mousey pointed!

With a great sob of disappointment Number 326 threw himself against the tiles. *What was that?* He listened with all his ears, fighting back the burning coughs. He could faintly hear the screams of a woman! "Sonia . . . Sonia!" he cried wildly, and unconsciously clutched at the agony in his throat. It was impossible to breathe in this air any longer.

"To the window . . . . to the window!" He thought he screamed the words but they were only a whisper. He staggered across the room and flung up the sash . . . . a gasp of air— real air! He turned to see the little detective crumple to the floor. Number 326 dragged him like a sack of meal to the window and draped him over the sill with his head outside, and he himself slumped in despair against the frame.

His eyes, raised hopelessly, suddenly gleamed anew. On the wall opposite was a fire emergency case. He shattered the glass with his bare fist. Blood spurted from his hand— unnoticed. He tore loose the axe and furiously attacked the tiled wall.

In the room beyond, Franz and the guard were fighting like demons for possession of the pistol. It was gripped in the hand of the guard whose wrist Franz clung to in a frenzy of strength; but slowly— slowly, the wrist turned the muzzle toward Franz's head. Suddenly the valet drew back, rammed his knee into his adversary's groin, snatched the pistol from the hand of the man convulsed in agony, and fired!

With one last effort, the guard rolled his body half around, ripped the hand grenade from his belt, and hurled it! But that last dying attempt failed. The bomb whirled to the far corner, and exploded there; the room rocked, a cloud of smoke and dust filled the air, followed by mortar and stone . . . . and cleared to show a great hole in the wall.

Caught by the force of the explosion, Number 326 had been hurtled across the room beyond. Stunned and bruised, blinded with pain and smoke and gas, his one thought was Sonia. He tried to get to his feet and tear through that opening, but his knees gave way— his legs refused to carry him.

Some one was picking his way through the smoking gap. It was Franz, returning to his master the girl who had been entrusted to him; returning her, if not entirely unharmed, yet still living and whole. Number 326, with a cry, tried to raise himself. He could hardly see, but he reached out his arms . . . . he touched her — and felt her arms about him.

"Here she is, sir," whispered Franz. "I kept my pledge, sir, as best I could. It— wasn't— easy.— I— was— forced— to speak— very rudely— to— Miss Sonia— I must— apologize. . . . . ."

All through his slow convalescence, Franz tried to puzzle out whether it had been a dream of the unconsciousness into the blackness of which he dropped, this memory of the touch of soft lips upon his torn and bleeding ones— this recollection of his master's arms about him, and his master's voice: "My faithful, loyal friend!"

CHAPTER XXIII

THE FINAL CLUE

HAGHI had disappeared.

The explosion that had blasted the walls had driven the gas with which the bank was filled into the inner recesses of the spy stronghold. Men and women had been smoked out like beasts from their lairs. Crawling out of their retreat, they had struggled to the fresh air through cellar trap-doors and secret openings, only to fall into the hands of the police. Unnerved and stunned, they had given themselves up in unconditional surrender, and offered no resistance as they were hauled away to jail in trucks.

But Haghi was not among them. They had been led before Sonia. She had scanned each face carefully, searching for the features of Haghi under some clever disguise. But, no— he was not among the prisoners. Haghi had escaped.

His picture was spread on every billboard; in the subways— on every fence— flashed on the screen in the movies, together with the notice of a great cash reward for his capture. Three faces were shown: that of President Haghi of Haghi's Bank— that of the Chief of the Spy Organization— and a third, that of a man whom no one had ever seen, his head, hair and eye-brows only sketchily indicated, no beard, but as in the other two showing those unmistakeable and brilliant eyes.

Number 326 had seen to it that these pictures of Haghi were broadcast throughout the country without delay; by the thousand they were despatched with amazing speed, flooding the country to the very frontiers. An army of motorcyclists and a battalion of planes scattered them. Every child on the streets became familiar with that sinister face, and Haghi's name was on everyone lips— yet, where was Haghi?

Discouraged and disheartened, Sonia, Miles Jason and Number 326 were sitting in the Chief's private office. Haghi's complete disappearance had cast a dark shadow on the otherwise unclouded happiness of the girl and man. The problem penetrated uncannily into every thought, every gesture— they were not free for a moment from that evil personality. It seemed to have

Stunned, they had surrendered without resistance.

wormed its way into every niche and corner of their lives.

The vilest tempers that Miles Jason had ever given vent to in all the many years of his life were sweet amiability compared to his present mood. He was on hair-trigger. The slightest word, the most harmless question, brought forth a violent explosion of rage. The capture of the stronghold, and the breaking up of the gang, had been a great success, to be sure, and had yielded much valuable material; but two things deprived the fiery Chief of any pleasure in the achievement: the first, the man he had set out to get had proved too clever for him; the second, the Treaty had not come to light, and the best they could hope for was that it had been burned, as had much other incriminating material, in the basement of the Spy Headquarters, when seizure was imminent.

Jason was storming up and down the room. That he was not smoking his pipe was an infallible sign that he was waiting for an opportunity to blow off some of the steam of his anger. Number 326 supplied the opportunity.

"A mouse couldn't escape from this city, let alone cross the frontier," he thought aloud.

The Chief turned on him like the enraged bull dog

he resembled. "You poor fool!" he roared, turning purple in the face, and stamping across the room on his short legs. "Haven't you learned a lesson yet? He escaped from the stronghold, didn't he? And wasn't that completely surrounded? And wasn't that more easy to guard than a whole city? Haven't you learned that that devil can see farther with his eye-*teeth* than you can with your eyes? Are you a hopeless idiot? Are . . . . Come in," he shouted, as a rap on the door interrupted his tirade.

The man who slipped through the door was sere and dry and thin enough to have been pressed in a book like an autumn leaf. Two frightened round eyes peered through a great pair of shell-rimmed glasses which covered nearly a third of his weazened face.

"What the hell do you want?" bellowed Jason.

Frightened the man might be, but so fired by the import of the news he was bringing that he held his ground. "I want to take the liberty of calling your attention, sir," he began nervously, "to a discrepancy that I cannot understand, sir."

"And is that a sufficient reason for disturbing me now?" roared the Chief.

"Yes, sir," replied the little clerk with an unusual firmness. "It's an entry I must make to-day, Mr. Jason.

It's about the numbers on those thousand pound notes which Number 326 gave me to enter."

"Well, and what of it? Are you suspecting Number 326 of holding out a few, perhaps, eh?"

"This is not a joke, sir. The numbers in the radiogram which Number 326 sent us wherein he asked us to trace the origin of the notes are quite different from the numbers actually on the money he handed over to me."

Jason and Number 326 stared first at the little man and then at each other. Suddenly Number 326 drew a sharp breath.

"Who received the radio I sent, sir?"

"I did."

"Was anyone with you when it came?"

"Yes— Number 719."

"Did he see the message?"

"Yes— Damn it all what are you driving at? He read the message to me. I couldn't find my glasses?"

"Did the message go out of your sight when 719 was in the office?"

"No . . . . yes it did. I tried to read it— couldn't — and threw it across the desk to him. It slipped onto the floor. He picked it up, read it and gave it back to me."

"Chief," said Number 326 slowly and seriously, "what could 719 have to gain by switching radiograms on you— giving you a false set of numbers?"

"Switching radiograms . . . . ! You're crazy, lad," exclaimed Jason.

"I think not, sir," replied Number 326 quietly. "You will find, I think, that 719 is the second member of your organization to double-cross you since I have been back."

"IMPOSSIBLE!" gasped the Chief.

"Not so impossible, sir, when you recall that 719 is also Nemo-the-Clown, and that it was Nemo-the-Clown who started me on the wrong track after that courier, and" he continued, driving home the words, "that it was Nemo-the-Clown who with so much kind forethought reserved that section for me in the *last* car— car number 33, 133."

With a great cry, Sonia sprang from her chair.

"HAGHI!" she screamed.

CHAPTER XXIV

THE LAST PERFORMANCE

NEMO-THE-CLOWN was on the stage at the Hippodrome. He was enjoying a very delightful evening. An audience of two thousand people were applauding him enthusiastically; he was in excellent form and in excellent spirits.

Nemo-the-Clown was playing a little nursery ditty on his absurd instrument— a curious thing, a fiddle with a horn. The audience, as usual were convulsed with laughter at his antics as he played.

A silent, grey-faced woman was occupying the fireman's niche. She was always to be seen there whenever Nemo-the-Clown was on the stage. Night after night she sat there alone, and looked in silence at Nemo-the-Clown. He never so much as glanced at her. Yet on one occasion, when the woman was absent, everyone who knew his act commented upon the nervousness that marred the performance.

SPIES

To-night the silent figure deserted her regular place. Her great stony eyes sought to catch those of Nemo-the-Clown, who either did not see, or refused to notice her.

Strange men had entered the wings. Speaking very quietly, they ordered everyone to move away. The acrobats, the trick cyclists, the toe dancer, and the clog dancers who were there watching Nemo's act, withdrew, much annoyed. They were greatly mystified, but the orders of these men were very definite and seemed backed by authority. One of the strangers stepped up to the silent woman, touched her lightly on the arm, and motioned her to leave also. She looked at him dully with her stony eyes. She refused to budge. They might drive everyone else away, but she would remain. The man hesitated, and walked off; he did not want to create a scene— just yet.

Nemo-the-Clown stepped down to the footlights. He spoke to the orchestra leader with his irresistible smile:

"A little soft music, please."

He tucked his distorted instrument under his chin, still smiling, although, as he turned from the orchestra, he had seen, half-concealed in the wings, two men each with a pistol trained directly on him. Nemo-the-

302

Clown glanced comically to the left and then to the right, tapping his foot to give the proper time to the orchestra. Men in both wings! "That's really too bad," he murmured to himself, and cut a ridiculously funny dance-step.

Then, with the orchestra in full swing, Nemo-the-Clown began to dance and sing and play. It was side-splitting, that dance in those grotesque shoes. He danced close to the wings— no chance at either side. He danced down to the footlights— there were three men in the orchestra pit who were keeping him covered both with their eyes and with their pistols— no chance. Nemo-the-Clown laughed aloud joyously, and his audience laughed with him.

Again, as his dance drew to a close, he passed the wings. "Aha! There's old Jason, and Number 326 . . . . both in at the death. But Sonia, Sonia . . . . that is another matter. Did you think that I would let another man have you . . . . no, no, my dear. . . . Now, Nemo-the-Clown is going to put on a new and sensational act! I wonder if you'll imitate it, Nemo, if you ever come out of the seclusion where I sent you because I needed your make-up, and your reputation. I haven't hurt the reputation, Nemo; in fact I think I have been the better clown of the two.

You'll find it hard to keep up to the standards I've
set. . . . . ."

A gigantic flea was pestering Nemo-the-Clown. He
fled from it— it pursued. He scratched himself violently, with his bow, with his fiddle, and then, hurling
these aside, with both hands. The flea leaped about
the stage, and Nemo sprang frantically after it. With
a desperate jump, he caught it, and as it struggled, he
pulled a pistol from his pocket and shot it. The flea,
seemingly only wounded, jumped for the wings.

To the audience, the glare of hate that distorted the
features of the clown was but comical anger at the
escaping flea. They roared with laughter, as he aimed
point blank at the girl in the wings and fired.

The shot missed, for Number 326 with a lightning-
like realization had hurled Sonia aside.

Nemo-the-Clown burst into harsh laughter. He
stared at his audience, and laughed again; he laughed
as though he would split his sides; and the audience
shouted in glee.

He stopped abruptly, and lifted the hand which held
the tiny pistol . . . a nice little plaything, eh what? So
you think it only a toy? Well. . . . . .

He put the muzzle against his bushy wig, and fired.

He swayed on his feet a moment, his huge shoes act-

ing as a support, then raising his hand, he called loudly:
"Curtain!"

Flat on his clown's face he fell, as the orchestra
swept into its final chords, and the curtain dropped
to the thunderous applause of the audience.

Miles Jason had rushed on the stage.

Number 326 caught Sonia in his arms. He covered
her tear-filled eyes with his hand.

The first to reach the side of the dying man was the
woman of the stony eyes— Petra. She dropped to
her knees, and refused to move, drawing the head of
Nemo-the-Clown close into her lap. She stared dully
at the people surrounding her, and at length she spoke,
she who had always passed as deaf and dumb, whom
none of them had ever heard utter a syllable:

"Let him die here, next to me— as he was born.
I am his mother."

EPILOGUE

SONIA freed herself suddenly from the arms of Number 326.

They were in that very room and upon the very couch of her "sanctuary," as Number 326 persisted in calling it. All her belongings had been found in the stronghold, and the little house was itself again.

She sat up very straight, and spoke with a mock severity:

"And do you suppose that I am willing to marry a man whose name I don't even know? That, sir, is ridiculous!"

Number 326 smiled, his face aglow with happiness:

"You fell in love with a nameless man, didn't you?"

The mock sternness fled, as she took his face between her hands and kissed him fiercely. "I did, my Beloved, I did!"

"But, yet, I suppose I *shall* have to tell you who I am. You *really* are interested in knowing? Then come here."

EPILOGUE

He leaned forward and whispered in her ear.

The girl started back, her eyes filled with a great amazement. "What . . . . !" she gasped.

Number 326 nodded.

THE END

Lightning Source UK Ltd.
Milton Keynes UK
16 March 2010
151495UK00001B/63/P